JAN 2012

For a moment he and Madeline simply stared at each other

She waited for him to say something. What? What the hell could he say? He didn't even know what to think right now.

The snow was melting into her hair, dampening it, making it start to curl. And then, when he was about to go back to the house—to a nightmare, no doubt—she said softly, "Have you ever heard of forgiveness, Ty?"

He couldn't bring himself to answer. He turned and walked away, leaving Madeline alone in the snow.

Dear Reader,

New York professor Madeline Blaine is a woman on a mission. The Nevada ranch she inherited two years ago isn't making money and she's determined to discover the reason why. Madeline doesn't know the first thing about ranching, but she fully intends to educate herself—on site. Ty Hopewell, her inherited ranching partner, has no idea how greatly his life is going to change once by-the-book Madeline arrives at the Lone Summit Ranch.

I love taking characters out of their comfort zones, and when Madeline arrives at the ranch, she not only has to learn about the realities of ranching—she has to learn how to manage without electricity for several hours a day, since the ranch generates its own power. This is a circumstance with which I am familiar, having lived off the grid for sixteen years. There are definite pluses to generating your own power, but there are also a few minuses. Generators, like automobiles, break down at the most inopportune moments. I've celebrated every major holiday without power because of generator malfunction—no lights, no water and, on one occasion, no turkey. On the plus side, my kids spent more time playing in the creek than watching television while growing up.

I had a great time writing about Madeline and Ty, and I hope you enjoy reading their story. I love to hear from readers, so please drop me a line at jeanniewrites@gmail.com or visit my website, www.jeanniewatt.com.

Happy reading,

Jeannie Watt

Maddie Inherits a Cowboy

Jeannie Watt

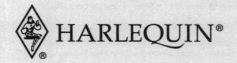

TORONTO • NEW YORK • LONDON
AMSTERDAM • PARIS • SYDNEY • HAMBURG
STOCKHOLM • ATHENS • TOKYO • MILAN • MADRID
PRAGUE • WARSAW • BUDAPEST • AUCKLAND

Recycling programs
for this product may
not exist in your area.

ISBN-13: 978-0-373-71690-6

MADDIE INHERITS A COWBOY

Copyright © 2011 by Jeannie Steinman

www.eHarlequin.com

Printed in U.S.A.

ABOUT THE AUTHOR

Jeannie Watt lives off the grid in the heart of Nevada ranching country. She and her husband share their acreage with horses and ponies, a dog, a cat and a wide assortment of wildlife. When she first moved to her off-the-grid locale she knew nothing about generators, but because the ancient propane-powered beast always acted up while her husband was at work, she learned. Before long she could change the oil and swap out points, plug and condenser in less than twenty minutes and was the family generator expert—the one the kids called when the generator sounded "funny." Now she has a new, more dependable generator, which she has wisely refused to learn about, leaving maintenance and care solely to her husband. So far, so good…but she dreams of solar power.

Books by Jeannie Watt

HARLEQUIN SUPERROMANCE

Don't miss any of our special offers. Write to us at the following address for information on our newest releases.

Harlequin Reader Service
U.S.: 3010 Walden Ave., P.O. Box 1325, Buffalo, NY 14269
Canadian: P.O. Box 609, Fort Erie, Ont. L2A 5X3

To my kids,
who grew up with the power going off
whenever their parents decided to go to bed.

To Roger,
who would drop everything and come to
my mechanical rescue when I got in over my head.

Thank you.

CHAPTER ONE

IT CAME UPON A midnight clear...

As soon as Ty Hopewell heard the familiar voice and recognized the opening bars of the song, he made a conscious effort to focus on his breathing, on the people passing in front of where he sat in the lobby of the Nugget Hotel and Casino. On anything except that song. He hadn't lived in the boonies for so long that he'd forgotten the day after Thanksgiving was the kickoff of the Christmas season. But he'd forgotten that every public place in Reno seemed to play music.

That glorious song of old...

Ty swallowed and then drew in a breath. He could do this. He could sit here and wait for his appointment. Or he thought he could, until he made the mistake of closing his eyes.

From angels bending near the earth...

Instantly he was lying on the frozen ground, disoriented and in pain. The truck was on its side, the cab caved in, the headlights cutting through the darkness at an angle that was just plain wrong.

The truck's front wheel slowly spun.

Bing Crosby sang.

For a moment it had been too much to process, and

then he'd realized that the radio in the demolished truck was still playing. Somehow. Bing's rendition of "It Came Upon a Midnight Clear" was the only sound in the cold desert night, so out of place in the aftermath of a violent wreck.

And then there had been another sound—his own voice screaming for his friend, demanding that Skip answer him….

Ty opened his eyes and got to his feet. He'd go outside, away from the music, to collect himself. Great plan, but he hadn't taken more than two steps when he saw her crossing the casino lobby. Madeline Blaine. Skip's sister.

It had to be her, since the time was exactly ten and she was wearing black slacks, a short red jacket and a black-and-white-checked scarf, exactly as she'd described on the phone the day before. She zeroed in on him, although she had no way of knowing what he looked like, and made a beeline toward him. Ty took off his hat as she approached.

"You must be Mr. Hopewell," she said briskly, extending her hand before he had a chance to speak. He took it briefly, knowing his own hand was probably ice-cold. It was the first time he'd met any of Skip's relatives. The funeral had taken place back east, where Skip had grown up.

"Yes. I'm Ty."

"Madeline."

He was struck by how little she looked like Skip. Her hair was straight and dark, while Skip's had been light brown and wavy. Her eyes were green; his had been brown. And Skip had been a big guy. His sister was on the small side, her features delicate. The only similarities he could see were the distinctive high cheekbones and fair skin. Skin that tended to fry under the Nevada sun. Skip had been forever sunburned.

She gestured at the chair where he'd been sitting a few seconds before. Ty obligingly sat and she took the chair kitty-corner to his, so they could face each other. Obviously Ms. Blaine was going to run this meeting. Ty just wanted it to be over. Hell, he wished he knew what it was about—and he wished Bing would shut up already, but the singer geared up for another verse.

Peace on the earth, goodwill to...

Ty ran a finger around the inside of his collar and Madeline Blaine tilted her head as she appraised him, a slight frown drawing her dark eyebrows together. "Are you all right?"

"Yeah. Fine." Except for the guilt that was crushing him as Bing sang. Technically, Skip's death had been an accident, but one that clearly could have been avoided if Ty hadn't been so damned stubborn.

He'd reached the point after twenty-three months where he didn't think about it as much—sometimes he could go several oblivious days at a time. But when he did think about Skip's death, it ate at him.

He looked into Madeline Blaine's clear green eyes, having no doubt about what had triggered him today. He hadn't been looking forward to this meeting with Skip's sister, and Bing hadn't helped matters.

He cleared his throat. "Ms. Blaine—"

"Dr. Blaine."

Oh-kay. She was a professor of anthropology at a small university somewhere in New York, but he hadn't realized he had to use her title. "*Dr.* Blaine."

"Madeline."

Ty took a deep breath. "I hope you didn't fly out here just to meet with me."

"Why else would I have come?" She spoke quickly, with unexpected defensiveness. Ty was a guy who watched people and picked up signals. The signal he was getting here he didn't quite understand.

"I thought you might have plans to do something else, to have some fun while you're here." Fun. Shit. Yeah, she should have fun while on a trip to settle her brother's estate. "What I mean is that there's stuff to do here in Reno."

Madeline sat a little taller. "I came to meet with you," she said, clasping her hands together. "About the ranch, as I'm sure you've surmised. The reasons we're losing money."

"We broke even this quarter," Ty pointed out. And they'd had this same discussion on the phone more than once. He understood her impatience, but the cattle market wasn't exactly booming right now—although organic beef was doing better than regular beef.

What he didn't understand was how flying across the country to meet with him face-to-face was going to help. To use the guilt factor perhaps? No matter how guilty he felt, it wouldn't make the cattle sales rebound any faster than they were.

But…whatever.

"The market is better than it was six months ago, yet that's not reflected in the ranch profits," Madeline said.

"There are things you need to understand." Things he'd thought he'd explained before, but for some reason Madeline wasn't getting it. "I've had to sink money into the ranch—money Skip would have had to sink into the ranch—to keep the infrastructure intact." He'd refenced the property and reroofed the barn, eradicated weeds, worked on the roads. The ranch wasn't in bad shape, but that was only because of the hours he'd put in after the accident, trying to forget the unforgettable.

Madeline nodded. Old news.

"Feed costs are up." Which was a double killer when cattle prices were down.

"I thought you raised your own hay," she said coolly.

"Not enough to feed the entire herd over the winter," Ty replied, still wondering why they were having this discussion in the lobby. Yet another carol played in the background. But at least this way they could get the meeting over with and Madeline could go about her business, whatever it might be. There was no way she'd flown across the country only to meet with him in a casino lobby.

"Then perhaps you need to plant more hay," Madeline said reasonably, as if pointing out a solution that had escaped him. But there was something in the tone of her voice that made Ty shift in his chair.

"The fields can only be irrigated during the spring because of the power and water situation, so that limits the amount of hay we can grow. And living off the grid, generating our own power, is expensive, what with ongoing generator maintenance and repairs and fuel."

She leaned back, studying him for a moment before saying, "I want to see the ranch."

Ty frowned. If he had known that, he would have sent photos. Real photos. The ones Skip had posted on his social websites had been misleading. They hadn't exactly shown anything except a spectacular view and cattle in the field. He'd probably sent his family the same pictures.

"In person," she added, reading his mind.

If Ty's teeth hadn't been clenched so tightly, his jaw would have dropped. "It's a five-hour drive."

"I've leased a car."

Leased? As opposed to rented? He felt a knot tightening in his stomach. "Look, Ms.… Dr.…." Ty gave up. "It's your right to come look at it, but I don't see how it's going to help. It's a long trip and then you'll just have to turn around and drive another hour and a half back to the closest town for the night."

"I plan to stay on the ranch."

Somehow he managed to say, "Why?" rather than "Are you nuts?"

Madeline pulled her shoulders back, making her posture even more upright. "Because I want to know exactly what's going on. I want to see how the operation runs and try to figure out why it isn't making money. Skip was no fool. If he went in with you, then the business, the property, must have had merit."

She was correct. Skip was no fool. But he'd been a romantic and thoroughly swept up in the cowboy mystique. Organic beef raised in an isolated environment off the grid appealed to him. "The property is good for what we wanted."

"Yet according to you, the property itself is part of the reason you're not making money."

"That and the market," he said grimly. He rested his forearms on his thighs, holding the brim of his black felt hat between his fingers as he met her eyes.

"The problems you've outlined are all problems Skip was dealing with when he was alive, and yet the ranch made money...*then*."

It was the way she emphasized the word *then* that finally clued Ty in.

"The ranch will make a profit again," he replied in a low voice, his expression stony.

Madeline drew in a breath through her nose, the action eloquently conveying her feelings on the matter, and Ty's back went up. He wasn't used to being treated as if he was trying to pull a fast one. A guy who'd caused an accident that had killed his friend, yes, but not a con artist.

He twisted his mouth as he debated, then he looked straight into her eyes and asked, "Did you fly here to accuse me of cheating you out of your half of the profits?"

She eyed him coolly. "Either that or mismanagement."

"Your accountant has the books."

She said nothing, but he could practically hear her asking, "Which set?"

He stood then, his hat in his hand. Reminding himself of her loss, of his culpability, he tried to hold in his temper. But Madeline Blaine didn't appear to be suffering over the loss of Skip. She seemed a lot more concerned about getting cash from the ranch. Well, that was her right. He owed her.

He also didn't like her.

"I'm not ripping you off."

She ignored the edge to his voice, which was a mistake.

"Unlike my brother, I tend to see the reality of situations without romanticizing them. I'm going to the ranch. I'm going to spend some time there and when I'm done, I'll know whether I need to audit, sell or hire someone to run my part of the business. Efficiently."

"Good luck with that," he said abruptly. Ty wasn't easily insulted, but this woman was taking wild swings at his integrity. "Keep me posted." Then he started for the stairs to the parking garage.

"Wait." He stopped and turned back. She was still standing next to the leather chairs. "You need to show me how to get there."

Ty stared at her for a second, then shook his head and started walking again. "You may as well show me," she said, catching up to him. "I'm going to spend the next several weeks there." She spoke as if he were foolish to ignore obvious logic.

"Then you'd better bring some food, lady, because I'm not sharing."

CHAPTER TWO

MADELINE WATCHED Ty Hopewell walk away, every inch the cowboy in his jeans, boots and burgundy wool jacket. And how appropriate that he wore a black hat over his dark hair. She didn't trust him. Not for one minute.

Skip had thought the world of him, but there was something fishy going on here. Why would the ranch make a decent profit right up until Skip's death? Her accountant had pointed out the vast amount of money Ty was pouring back into the ranch, which cut the profits down to nothing, but neither of them knew whether the expenditures were necessary...or even happening.

Madeline lived two thousand miles away. Ty could say he was doing a lot of things, but whether or not he was—that was the question. If he was benefiting from her brother's death and cheating her in the process, it was going to stop. If he merely stank at managing the place, that had to be addressed as well, and thanks to an unfortunate twist of fate, she was free to look into the matter.

At least some small bit of good would come from her suspension.

Her temples throbbed at the thought. Madeline was

a consummate rule-follower, and being suspected of illegally misappropriating data in her boss's groundbreaking study was killing her. There was nothing she could do until the formal investigation was completed, except to drive her legal counsel, Everett, crazy, so here she was. With Everett's blessing and wishes of Godspeed, she'd decided to channel her considerable energies into understanding exactly why her inheritance was no longer making money.

And…if she chose to take the chicken's way out, to lie low at the ranch until this brouhaha at work was over, so what? She owned half the blasted property. She was entitled.

She stalked back through the lobby, past the Starbucks with green metallic garlands strung along the counter, past the reception desk with the tasteful winter floral arrangements. Christmas music played over the speaker system, music that always made her feel closer to Skip. He'd died on Christmas Eve, and sometimes it was almost as if he was speaking to her through the songs.

Tidings of comfort and joy…

She didn't feel much joy, but she did feel comfort.

Or she had until her confrontation with Ty.

Where was he now? Leaving the parking garage on his way to "the ranch"? The place didn't even have a name, as far as she knew. Having been born and raised in Syracuse, she wasn't all that ranch savvy, but didn't all ranches have names? The Lazy M or the Flying L or some such thing?

Skip would have known. Skip had not only thrown himself into studying the West, he'd thrown himself into the culture. He'd been bound and determined to be a cowboy.

Madeline swallowed a lump in her throat as the elevator doors slid open. She pushed the key card into the slot and then punched in her floor number. Every now and then grief still hit her, but she'd been expecting it this time because of the circumstances. She wished for the zillionth time that Skip had never met Ty Hopewell, had never gone into the cattle business with him.

At first she'd blamed Ty for Skip's death, but after studying the accident report had concluded, as had the highway patrol, that it was simply an unfortunate accident involving a cow on a dark highway. Eventually she'd shoved her feelings of blame aside. Skip was gone. She could honor him best by enjoying the memories she had of him.

The doors opened and she walked down the hall to her room to gather her bags and check out. The only reason she wasn't hot on Ty Hopewell's tail right now was because she wasn't the type who left her key in the room and had her invoice emailed to her. No. She liked to check out in person, examine the bill and then leave with a hard copy in her hand. No mistakes that way.

She sat on the edge of the bed, then after a few seconds lay back on the brocade bedcover, her feet still hanging over the side, toes dangling above the floor. Her no-mistakes era was over. She stared up at the ceiling, not caring for once if she wrecked her perfectly flatironed hair. She'd tried so hard not to make errors in any area of her life. To cross her t's and dot her i's. To cover her ass and more than that, to make certain she never had anything to cover her ass for. And what happened?

Her trusted mentor was accused of academic misconduct that threatened federal funding to Wilcox University, that's what. And, as Dr. Jensen's former associate, she was being sucked into the undertow.

Madeline hadn't been involved—she'd known nothing about the blood samples Dr. Jensen had used without permission for research into the origins of indigenous peoples—but she'd worked so closely with him on his previous projects that she had to be investigated, too. Or at least that was the explanation given when she'd been put on leave. Madeline didn't buy it for a second.

It was obvious to her that the new anthropology department head, Dr. Vanessa Mann, was indulging in revenge, since Madeline had the unfortunate tendency to speak out when she disagreed with policies and procedures. As soon as she'd taken over the department, Dr. Mann had begun emphasizing research over education. Research brought in money, but the college was supposed to educate, for heaven's sake. It was absolutely wrong to have the majority of classes taught by graduate students and teaching assistants while the tenured professors holed up in their offices.…

Madeline stopped herself.

She'd felt safe speaking out since she'd had justified concerns. The result? Well, she was living the result.

Someone else was teaching her classes. Someone else was guiding her graduate students. And Dr. Mann had made it look like a necessary action that had been taken as part of an important investigation.

Madeline squeezed her eyes shut, felt the heat rising in her cheeks. Even after two weeks she was so damned embarrassed.

She forced her eyes open again.

She needed to pack. She needed to figure out how to get to this ranch with no name. She had a full day ahead of her and no time to feel sorry for herself.

EVERY NOW AND THEN Ty found himself glancing into the rearview mirror and checking the traffic behind him on the freeway to see if he was being followed. Which was ridiculous, since he'd been on the interstate within five minutes of leaving the annoying Dr. Blaine in the lobby of the Nugget. There was no way she was on his tail, and even if she was, he had no idea what she was driving, so he couldn't have spotted her, anyway.

I'm going to stay on the ranch.... His lips twisted. For a night maybe. Until reality set in. She didn't look like the type who would embrace life off the grid. He'd made a tactical error, though, by letting his anger get the best of him, and walking away. He should have let her follow him to the ranch, see what the property was like, assure herself that there was a ranch—that he wasn't embezzling funds or equipment or pretending to buy things he hadn't.

But when she'd pretty much said he was either

dishonest or stupid, with those Christmas carols playing in the background...well...he wasn't at the top of his game. So what now? They were still business partners. He couldn't exactly go back and find her. But he could call her. Apologize for being insulted by her unfounded insinuations. Try to do some damage control.

Hell. Whatever it took to get this issue settled. He fumbled for his phone as he drove, but when he dialed her number, there was no answer. He dropped the phone back on the seat beside him. Oh, well. He'd tried. Ty glanced in the mirror again, caught himself, cursed and focused on the road ahead.

The turnoff to Fallon was coming soon. Three more hours and he'd be home. Hell of a long drive to make, only to be pissed off. Now he had to consider what he was going to do when Madeline showed up, because, barring a blizzard—which to his disappointment wasn't in the offing—he had no doubt she'd find her way to the ranch.

Skip had often spoken of his sister's tenacity in a fond way. Ty was going to experience that tenacity up close and personal.

AFTER A FEW MINUTES on the internet, using the geographical coordinates from the legal documents, Madeline had both a map and the name of the road the ranch was on. Lone Sum Road. She stared at the screen, wondering if she was looking at a typo or if this was Western cleverness. Lone Sum. Lonesome?

Whatever.

She printed the map on her portable printer and then loaded her bags on the folding luggage dolly she never traveled without. Some of her associates teased her about the tubular steel device on wheels—but never when they were battling their own luggage.

Madeline's larger suitcases were still in the car. She hadn't bothered to bring them in, since she'd assumed she'd be following Ty Hopewell to the ranch. After making her suspicions known, she hadn't expected him to be enthusiastic, but she hadn't expected him to simply drive away, either.

Which left the question of whether he'd merely been insulted by her direct approach or did he have something to hide?

She'd soon find out.

As she traveled east, her cellular service popped in and out, mostly out, so she was surprised when she got a call. It was Connor, her research assistant and the only person, according to Skip, who was more of a tight ass than she was—which was why Madeline was glad she had him. If she forgot some detail, she was certain Connor would catch it.

"Where are you?"

Madeline took in the barren landscape. "Quite literally in the middle of nowhere. I'm driving to the ranch. It's more than four hours from Reno."

"I tried to call three times."

"Bad service here. You should see this place. Mountains and flat. That's it. I've driven for more than thirty miles without seeing a house." Madeline shifted the phone to her other ear. "What's happening there?"

"Nothing on the professional front, but I went to visit your grandmother."

"How is she?"

"Rambunctious." Madeline felt a surge of relief. *Rambunctious* meant no bronchial relapse. "There's been complaints from the apartment next door. Loud music—"

"She's losing her hearing."

"Parties."

"Give me a break." Connor might be a detail guy, but he had a sense of humor.

"I tried to talk her into the iPod again, but no luck. She refuses to wear headphones."

"Well, as long as she doesn't get kicked out." Grandma Eileen, also a professor of anthropology, lived in a retirement complex that catered to the academic set. She was seventy-two years old and very active. Madeline's many cousins made sure she was never lonely, but it was Madeline and Skip that had a special bond with Eileen, who'd taken them in when their parents divorced and went to find themselves on different continents. Her grandmother was also the reason Madeline had been able to make peace with what had happened to her brother.

Grieve now or grieve later, Eileen had said, but she wanted Madeline to understand that she wasn't going to escape the process. She hadn't escaped, but after a year she had reached acceptance. The stage where she could remember Skip without sharp pain.

"Thanks for taking my visit," Madeline said. Connor, who had next to no family of his own, considered himself one of the grandkids, so she knew it was no chore. "Are you sure there's no news on the Jensen front?"

"Noth—" A sharp beep cut off Connor's reply. No signal. Madeline snapped the phone shut.

An hour later she pulled into Winnemucca for gas. It was hard to believe she was still in the same state and that she'd passed through only two towns of any size since leaving Reno. The emptiness, the vastness of this land, was daunting. Not only that, it was damned cold and snowy. This was not the desert she'd envisioned from her brother's enthusiasm about his new home. The mountains were pretty, much more rugged and barren than the ones she was used to, but other than that, what had Skip seen in this country?

Madeline adjusted her collar against the wind and screwed the gas cap on. According to the GPS, she had another hundred and eighty miles—and two more towns—to go before reaching her target destination.

She was nearing the town of Battle Mountain when it began to snow, and during the sixty mile drive to Elko what should have been an hour's drive turned into an hour and a half.

Ty might have been angry when he'd told her to bring food, but Madeline took him at his word. As soon as she hit Elko, she stopped and bought a bag of groceries—mostly cereal and cookies. Carbohydrates fed the brain.

When she left the store, she was glad to see that the skies were clearing, although there was a good six inches of unplowed snow on the road. She loaded the groceries into the car and wearily got back in. She wasn't exactly looking forward to reaching the ranch, but she was looking forward to not driving anymore. It had been one long day. And it was only half over.

THERE WAS NO WAY in hell that a car, even one with all-wheel drive, should have made it up Lone Summit Road after a snowfall. But damned if Madeline Blaine didn't climb out of a Subaru Outback and wade through the drift to the gate at the end of the driveway.

Ty tipped back the brim of his black felt hat and watched from the corral where he'd just fed the bulls. A full minute later he knew he had to go help her. What kind of a person could navigate that road and then not be able to figure out a gate latch? Apparently one with a doctorate in anthropology.

He muttered a curse and trudged down the snowy drive with Alvin, his border collie, at his heels, walking in the same track Ty created. She was obviously het up to see the ranch, so see the ranch she would. He had a feeling when she was done that she was going to wish she'd believed him.

Madeline did not give up on the latch. She continued to wrestle with it right up until he stopped on the opposite side of the gate.

"Need help?" he asked mildly.

"What do you think?" she snapped.

You don't want to know what I think.... "I'm surprised you made it," he said after he pulled the mechanism that released the latch—the mechanism that Madeline had been pushing for all she was worth. She lifted her chin slightly when she saw how easily the latch sprang open.

"What do you mean?"

"The snow, the ruts, the road."

She made a face. "I grew up in New York. I can drive in the snow and I don't need one of those to do it." She pointed at his four-wheel-drive pickup truck parked next to the barn a hundred yards away.

"Bully for you," he muttered as she trudged back to her car and got inside. He and Alvin stood clear as she drove past, and then Ty shut the gate. Madeline had parked next to the truck and was out of the car, standing in the snow, when he and Alvin caught up with her.

"I'll show you Skip's house."

"Thank you."

She followed him as he broke trail through the calf-deep snow to the double-wide closest to the barn. Skip had lived in the newer of the two prefab ranch houses. Both were roomy, with three bedrooms and two baths and, under normal circumstances, quite comfortable. These were not normal circumstances, though. Skip's place had been uninhabited for almost two years and Ty had a feeling Madeline wasn't going to find the place all that inviting. Oh, well. He'd told her not to come.

Ty walked up the stairs and opened the door.

Madeline stalled out at the bottom step. "I assume there are no mice inside? It has been empty for some time."

He had managed to keep the mice out so far—no small feat in the country—with a lot of caulk and steel wool. He figured that if he ever expanded to the point that he could hire help, or if he got another partner to buy into the operation, he'd need to keep the house up.

Perhaps that had been a mistake.

"No mice. I check frequently." It was still hard for him to go inside Skip's place, and cleaning it out had been a hell he never wanted to have to repeat.

Madeline slowly climbed the stairs with a suitcase in each hand. Her concern about mice only reinforced his belief that she wasn't going to last long at the ranch, but he had to give her credit for not flinching at the amount of fine silt that had worked its way in through the edges of the windows and settled. One of the joys of desert life—even in the high country.

The only furniture in the two front rooms was a leather sofa that pulled out into a bed—in case Ty had company who wanted privacy, which was laughable because Ty never had company—and a small kitchen table with two chairs. The other rooms were empty. Everything had been shipped home or sent to charity.

"I sent the bedding and towels and stuff to Good-will."

"I know," she said briskly. She walked through the house, the floor squeaking beneath her steps. "I brought a sleeping bag."

"You're really staying."

Her eyebrows lifted, as if in surprise, but the reaction seemed forced—quite possibly because of *where* she would be staying. The house was not inviting. "I told you I was."

"Suit yourself." The sooner she saw that everything was on the up-and-up, the sooner this walking, talking reminder of Skip would be out of his life.

"I will." She glanced around and from the way she moistened her lips he had a feeling she was fighting to keep her placid expression. She brought her eyes back to his face.

"Not much to do here," Ty explained. "No TV or anything."

"I plan to use any free time I might have to work on a book I'm writing."

Ty stared at her. "How long do you plan to stay?" he asked, his voice hoarse.

"Three and a half weeks."

Oh, shit. Why didn't she just take out a gun and shoot him?

This went beyond not wanting to be reminded about Skip. Ty enjoyed his solitude. Hell, he embraced it. When he wanted company he went to town. He did not want it forced on him.

Madeline squared her shoulders. "Well, I guess I'll go and get the rest of my luggage. I have a busy afternoon."

Ty nodded and headed for the door. There wasn't much else he could do.

CHAPTER THREE

GOOD HEAVENS, SKIP, what were you thinking when you bought this place?

He'd said it was isolated, but Madeline couldn't believe how far she'd driven on that darned Lone Sum Road before finally seeing the driveway and gate. Beyond the gate she'd recognized the view from the photos Skip had sent, but when Skip had talked of a ranch, she'd envisioned a big wooden barn and sheds and lots of board fences and corrals. Well, the barn was there. It was big and metal and ugly. The smaller buildings all looked as if they were a couple hundred years old, and the fences were made of wire. Wire.

She thought he'd sent pictures of the view because it was so spectacular. She hadn't realized there was nothing else to photograph.

Ty had disappeared and was hopefully hooking up the electricity, while Madeline carried her belongings into the frigid house, which was larger than she had expected. Skip had called it a trailer, but it was the size of a regular house with a woodstove on a ceramic-tiled hearth.

She made three trips through the snow between her car and the house, leaving the door propped open. The last trip was the easiest because she'd beaten the snow into a path. Then she took another look at her living quarters.

She should have bought more cleaning supplies.

And a bucket.

Madeline pulled a pad out of her purse and started a list, then went to the sink and turned the tap. Nothing.

So she wouldn't be cleaning and she wouldn't have heat until Ty got around to turning on the power. Perhaps Mr. Hopewell needed a nudge. Madeline had no intention of disturbing him any more than she had to during her stay, but she also had no intention of freezing to death.

She stepped outside, debating whether it was warmer inside or outside, then followed Ty's tracks to the barn.

When she opened the door, Ty looked up from the contraption he was working on. He had a smudge of oil across his cheek and he seemed none too happy to see her. Or maybe he was ticked off at the machine…which was probably the generator.

Madeline had a feeling it was.

Ty shifted his scowl back to the machine. "It hasn't been started in a while."

"Will it start?" Because if not, she was on her way back down the mountain to the little town at the bottom. Except that she hadn't seen anyplace to stay there.

"Hope so."

"Does it have fuel?" Madeline asked.

No answer this time, so she concluded it was a stupid

question. But she'd also learned during the course of her academic career at the university never to overlook the obvious.

Ty replaced the metal cover and tightened a wing nut. He put his finger on a toggle switch next to a gauge, then paused a second.

Madeline thought he was probably praying it wouldn't start, but decided to give him the benefit of the doubt. He flipped the switch and the machine began to shake as it chugged to life. And then the chug turned into a roar and the shaking turned into a steady vibration. Madeline automatically placed her hands over her ears and retreated out of the building. Ty followed, closing the door behind him and muting the sound. A little.

"Loud," Madeline said as she dropped her hands.

"Welcome to life on a generator." He started for Skip's house and she followed. He stepped inside and went to the hallway, where he opened the furnace door and started banging around. A few seconds later a blast of heat shot out of the register next to Madeline. She stepped on top of it, sighing as the warmth blew up her pant legs.

"How about the water?"

"I'll turn it on and get the hot-water heater going. Then…you're on your own, although I have no idea what you're going to do."

"I'm going to clean this place up tonight, and tomorrow we're going to meet."

"What if it doesn't work into my schedule?"

"Then you'd better fit me in, unless you do have

something to hide." Madeline said it without thinking, then instantly regretted it when Ty slowly turned back to her.

"You're not much like your brother, are you?" Madeline opened her mouth to reply but before she could say anything, Ty added, "I never saw Skip go for the jugular like you do."

She was *not* going for the jugular. She was being truthful.

"Maybe if Skip had been more like me, he wouldn't have been in business with you and he wouldn't…" Her voice trailed off. Ty swallowed—she saw his Adam's apple move—then left the house without another word.

Madeline stared at the door. She wasn't sure what exactly had gotten into her, but was beginning to suspect, now that she'd met Ty, that she still wanted to blame him for Skip's death.

SHE WASN'T THE LEAST BIT like her brother in temperament or in coloring, true, but there were similarities. Facial expressions, the cadence of her speech, the faint accent.

Except, regardless of what she said, Ty was right. She did go for the jugular. She pinpointed his weakest point and then thrust in the knife. She'd done it twice now—stabs at his honesty and stabs at his integrity. He had no doubt she'd twist the knife, too, if he gave her the chance. She looked the type, all high-and-mighty and so sure she was right.

Alvin followed him to the house, then glanced up at him when Ty opened the door.

"Yeah, you're sleeping inside."

Alvin preferred to sleep outside, but Ty wanted the company tonight. His house was equipped with a cabin kit, a switch inside for his generator, which was newer, quieter, more fuel efficient than the one powering Skip's place.

It rumbled to life in its shed behind his house and the lights came on. Ty went over to his desk and turned on the computer. He had to turn down that specialty-foods company toeing into the organic market. He wouldn't be able to supply as much beef as they wanted. Because of the demand for hormone-free, antibiotic-free beef— despite a market recession—he was actually doing all right. But he wasn't able to supply volume. Yet. That's why the money went into his herd, equipment and ranch improvements. He needed to expand. Skip's idea, really. Skip had been a financial whiz kid and a good business partner.

Madeline, not so much.

But she was fully within her rights being here, taking a look at the property, living in Skip's house. Hell, she could live there forever. But Ty was within his rights not to work on that damned antique generator when it went down. That was her concern.

Ty pulled a cast-iron pan out from under the stove and flicked on a burner, trying not to look out the window at the lights in Skip's house. Lights that hadn't been on for almost two years. If he'd known how all this was going to work out, he would have bought two cows, ten acres and continued to work at the feedlot.

IT TOOK ALMOST AN HOUR for the hot-water tank to do its job. Madeline was too impatient to wait, so she started cleaning with paper towels and water, pretty much making mud on the silty counters during her first swipes, and then after rinsing the thankfully strong paper towels, eventually getting the surfaces clean.

Once the counters were done, Madeline regarded the floors, also silt-covered. When she'd first set foot in the house, she'd wondered why there was no carpeting. She didn't wonder anymore. Carpet would be a commando dust trap, even with a supervacuum.

Right now she wished she had a SuperVac. Or a broom.

Madeline pressed a hand to her forehead, then went to the counter where her cell phone was plugged in, for all the good it would do. She turned it on and found that it was still searching for a signal. Crap. She knew there'd been a signal at the turnoff for Lone Sum Road, because she'd talked to her grandmother, fending off questions about why she wasn't finishing the semester at the college. Eileen knew about Dr. Jensen, but Madeline hadn't yet broken the news that she, too, was under investigation. Connor and her cousins were under strict orders not to let it slip. Madeline didn't want her grandmother worrying about her, so she'd intimated that she had a grad student who needed teaching experience, thus freeing her to take care of business at the ranch. Eileen had more questions, but fortunately Madeline lost the signal as she started up Lone Sum Road. It had been a good thing, too, since the last few miles had required all of her attention.

She turned off the phone, set it back on the counter. Apparently if she wanted to make a call to Connor for moral support, she was going to have to drive to the bottom of the mountain to do it. Not tonight. She walked over to where her suitcases sat on the dusty floor. She didn't want to open them for fear of getting dust on everything in them, so instead she paced to the curtainless window and stared out at the lights of Ty's house, a hundred yards away. The ranch was set up so that they had their privacy. Skip's house was close to the barn and Ty's close to the gate.

And both houses close to nothing else. The only sound was the generator, the source of her power, chugging away. How was she supposed to sleep with that noise?

Skip? Explanation, please? How did you handle this? Why did you handle this?

She probably wouldn't be sleeping, so she might as well be cleaning. To do that she needed a few things Ty probably had. Madeline pulled on her coat and headed for the door.

The generator was louder outside. She didn't have a flashlight, and the ranch had no yard light, so she made her way to Ty's house by moonlight reflecting off the snow. When she got there, she knocked and was greeted by loud, serious barking.

A second later Ty opened the door, his dog regarding her suspiciously from behind the man's long legs.

Madeline tilted her chin up. "May I please borrow a broom?"

Ty's mouth tightened and then he nodded. He left the door open as he crossed to a utility closet in the kitchen. Madeline hesitated, then stepped inside, keeping her eye on the less-than-friendly-looking dog. Weren't collies supposed to be friendly?

"And a dustpan?" she called when Ty pulled out a broom.

He reached back into the closet, pulling out a dustpan, along with a mop and bucket. He set the bucket on the floor and thrust the cleaning implements at her.

"Anything else?" he asked in an expressionless voice.

"Cleaner?"

He didn't say a word as he went to a kitchen cabinet and pulled out a bottle of 409. He walked back to where she stood, guarded by his dog, and dropped the bottle in the bucket. It landed with a small thunk.

Madeline squared her shoulders. The guy did not like her. The message was oh-so clear in his closed-off body language, his refusal to speak. Well, she had invaded what he probably, erroneously, thought of as his turf. In a way, she understood his reaction, but it wasn't going to have any effect on her behavior toward him.

After she had gathered the cleaning supplies and stepped back out onto the porch, he finally said, "If you're going to clean tonight, you'd better hurry."

She turned back with a frown. "Why?"

"You have half an hour before I turn off the generator."

"I have what?" She really hoped her jaw didn't drop.

"Half an hour. We don't have enough fuel to run your generator full-time, and frankly, it's too old to run full-time."

"Does your power go off, too?" she demanded. Over his shoulder she noticed a computer sitting on the desk, a search-engine screen clearly visible. He had internet. She couldn't even get a cell signal.

"Of course," he said, and although his expression remained passive, she had a feeling he was enjoying this.

"When do you turn the power back on?"

"In the morning for a few hours. Do you have a flashlight?"

"In my car," Madeline said in a faint voice as she weighed the ramifications of this new and unexpected information.

"Don't plan on using a lot of water while the gen's off. No power, no pump."

Her eyes flashed up to his face. "Excuse me?"

"You have a water storage tank, but it's not huge. Don't take a shower or anything."

For the second time that night Madeline was left staring at a closed door.

Was he being serious? Or inventing rules to make her miserable?

If he was... If he was, Madeline had no way of finding out. She was in over her head here, but damned if she was going to cry uncle.

She lifted her hand and pounded on the door. For a second she didn't think he would answer, but he did, swinging it open, a harsh expression on his face.

"What?" he asked in a deadly voice.

"Would you give me some warning before you turn off the electricity?" Madeline said calmly, making Ty feel like a jerk for growling at her. But damn it, he wasn't used to having other people around, insulting his integrity, then knocking on his door and borrowing cleaning supplies.

The sane thing to do would be to teach her how to operate the generator so she could turn the power on and off herself. It was hers, after all, but no one within sixty miles worked on the machines, so if it went down, it could be down for days. In the dead of winter. That wasn't an option. He didn't want her trying to move in with him.

"I'll knock on your door. You don't need to answer. Just get into bed before the lights go out."

"Thank you." Madeline gathered her supplies and trudged off down the path through the snow to Skip's house, the mop bobbing as she walked. Ty watched her for a moment before closing the door.

When he went back to his work—a rural development grant for pasture improvement—he couldn't concentrate. He doubted he'd be able to focus as long as Skip's sister was on the property, and that wasn't good, since she appeared to be putting down roots.

Ty waited until he couldn't stay awake any longer before letting himself out into the cold to turn off Madeline's generator. The porch steps clunked under his boots as he climbed. He gave two loud raps, then turned and retraced his steps, hands thrust deep in his pockets. He hadn't bothered to put on gloves. He didn't want to talk to Madeline and he didn't trust her not to open the door and either ask a question or make an observation. Sure enough, he heard the door open behind him, but pretended he didn't. A second later, it closed again. Bullet dodged.

He waited in the barn for a couple minutes to give her time to settle, then flipped the toggle on the generator. The house went dark. He hoped Madeline had gone straight to bed, as he'd suggested. But he had a sneaking suspicion, given the flashlight beam arcing through the interior of the house, that she hadn't.

Welcome to life off the grid.

CHAPTER FOUR

OKAY, SKIP. I WANT ANSWERS.

Madeline burrowed deeper into the sleeping bag she'd laid out on the leather sofa. She hadn't folded the couch out into a bed, for fear of the amount of dust she might find inside. She hadn't started cleaning, either, not wanting to suddenly find herself in the dark. But for some reason, Ty had waited almost an hour before turning off the electricity. Wasted time.

She wasn't sure what exactly she'd expected when she got to the ranch, but it wasn't this—a dusty, empty double-wide with intermittent electricity. When Skip had said they generated their own power on the ranch, she'd had a romantic vision of solar panels and twenty-four-hour-a-day electricity.

Madeline was tough. She had generations of Yankee blood flowing through her veins. But over those generations, the Yankees had become accustomed to showering whenever they pleased and lighting rooms with a flip of a switch. She was slightly ashamed for needing those things when she prided herself on being up to any challenge, but it was the twenty-first century. Native American tribes at the bottom of the Grand Canyon had electricity and internet.

She'd certainly be talking to Ty about the power situation. Why didn't the ranch have solar power? Or wind generators instead of these diesel monstrosities? Cost was undoubtedly an issue, but had he even looked into it before spending so much money on the ranch? Was he unaware of the benefits of twenty-four-hour electricity?

If Madeline had been able to see, she would have made a note.

A melancholy moan from somewhere outside the double-wide brought Madeline upright in her sleeping bag, hands clutched to her chest. Her eyes, which had been drifting shut, were now wide-open as she stared into the darkness, listening.

What on earth…?

The plaintive bawl came again, sending a shiver up her spine before she realized the sound had to be coming from…a cow? Of course. Ranch. Cow.

That sound was nothing like a moo. Not even close, but it had to be a cow.

Madeline slowly settled back down into the bag, her heart still beating a little faster. The house was cooling off at warp speed now that the heat source was gone, so she pulled the soft nylon up to her cheekbones and thought about putting on her ski hat. She'd have to see about getting wood.

Or go home.

The thought shot from out of nowhere and Madeline quickly dismissed it. She'd made plans and she was following through. Besides, her lawyer was glad to have her on the other side of the country and not calling every day with a new angle of attack for her defense.

She flopped over and pulled the bag up over her head, risking a headache from lack of fresh air, but her nose was getting cold.

Toughen up.

If Skip could handle living this way, then so could she.... Although when they were kids, Skip's idea of a good time was camping in the swampy area behind the house and coming back cold, wet, dirty and tired. She'd preferred to curl up with a book and lose herself in another world while the rain beat on the windows.

The thought of being out in the rain, battling the elements, had never appealed to her, just as living in the middle of nowhere didn't appeal. She had a fiscal responsibility, however, to herself and to her grandmother, so she would muscle through the unexpected physical discomfort and learn something about this ranch she owned half of.

She'd also...hopefully...keep her mind occupied and stop driving herself crazy with what-ifs about her career.

TY WOKE UP SHORTLY BEFORE dawn. He stared into the darkness for a moment, letting his eyes adjust, before rolling onto his back and flopping an arm over his face. He felt like shit. The cold hopelessness that had engulfed him for so many months after the accident was back. In spades.

No. He was wrong. It wasn't the same. There was a

sense of foreboding mixed in with the usual guilt and darkness. Ty ran a hand over the back of his neck, which was about as stiff as it had been for two weeks after the wreck, when he hadn't been able to turn his head.

Damn it, Skip, I'm sorry. I know you were fond of her, but I just can't warm up to your sister.

Alvin poked his cold nose against Ty's shoulder and he automatically ruffled the dog's silky fur before shoving the blankets aside and getting out of bed. He shivered as he walked naked into the kitchen to turn on the generator and get some heat flowing. He went to the door and let Alvin out, realizing only as he was shutting it that perhaps he shouldn't do that naked anymore—at least not while Madeline was on the property. Not that she could see much at that distance, but no sense taking chances or prompting complaints.

How long was she going to stay? For real, that was, after she became acquainted with the actuality of life on Lone Summit Ranch. Days, he hoped. He should be so lucky.

The smartest thing for him to do would be to give her whatever information she needed. Answer her questions, weather her insults, show her whatever she wanted to see and do it ASAP. Starting this morning. Then maybe she'd leave.

That was the plan, anyway, but after eating a quick breakfast of coffee and toast with peanut butter, he couldn't bring himself to knock on Madeline's door and ask her when she wanted to go over whatever it was she wanted to go over. Instead he walked past the double-wide to the barn, where he started the tractor. Once it was running and he was ready to pull out and drive to the hay shed, he turned on her generator, holding his breath as always. The ancient machine coughed and chugged, then took hold.

Duty done, he adjusted the scarf around his neck and pulled his earflaps down, then climbed into the driver's seat. Alvin was already waiting on the empty flatbed trailer. He gave two barks, his way of communicating approval that at long last they were starting the real work of the day. As Ty put the tractor in gear, the little collie braced himself, his sharp gaze darting here and there as he guarded his trailer against any marauders that might try to hitch a ride.

MADELINE'S EYES FLASHED open as the overhead lights came on. Normally she never slept this late—it was almost 8:00 a.m. eastern standard time—but she hadn't fallen asleep until very, very late. In fact, she'd resigned herself to staring up at the dark ceiling, her nose getting colder as the temperature steadily dropped, and wondering if Skip had truly enjoyed living this way or had been too proud to admit he'd made a mistake.

Somewhere along the line, she'd fallen asleep.

She sat up and then immediately snuggled back into the sleeping bag. The room was even more frigid than when she'd fallen asleep, but the furnace had come on with the power. She would let the heat blow for a few minutes.

Or a few hours.

Madeline compromised and climbed out of the bag ten minutes later and put on her coat. She hurried to the bathroom and shut the door to trap the heat flowing up through the vents. Blessed warmth.

Having no idea how long the electricity would be on—something else to discuss with Ty—she cranked on the shower, grimacing slightly as the water ran rusty. It cleared after a few minutes and she climbed under the wonderfully strong spray, letting it beat on her shoulders and back, warming her.

Madeline stood under the shower until the water started to cool—something she rarely did, but she had a slightly larger water tank back home. She stepped out into the saunalike environment she'd created, cleared the condensation off the mirror with her washcloth, then prepared for the daily battle with the blow-dryer and flatiron.

Once that was done, she would brew a thermos of instant coffee, then sit down with her laptop and write up a plan of attack for the morning and afternoon. She'd spend the evening working on her great-grandmother's memoir, with a flashlight if necessary.

First on the list—set up a meeting with Ty. She hoped today he was in a mood to cooperate.

Second—a trip back down the mountain. She wanted to talk to Connor, both to touch base and to vent about the state of this alleged ranch, her uncertainties concerning Ty. She needed a sounding board. Someone she could trust.

THE MORNING WAS NOT going well. Fair or not, Ty blamed Madeline. If she hadn't come to the ranch, he would have been able to concentrate. He wouldn't have hit the pothole under the snow, shifting his load of hay so that he caught a bale on the gatepost as he drove through.

After he'd restacked the hay, Alvin held the cows off while Ty opened the second gate, the one leading to the cattle pasture, and drove the tractor through. The dog leaped back onto his trailer and Ty started feeding without incident, Alvin happily snapping and barking at the cows to keep them from pulling bales off one side of the trailer while Ty dropped hay off the other. But while Ty usually found a temporary sense of peace in the simple act of feeding, today a dark cloud hung over him.

Were these his only choices in life? To be depressed or to be angry?

Hell of a way to live.

Man up. Madeline was Skip's sister. His inherited business partner. He had to do his duty and be civil. She was here for answers he owed her, to clear up suspicions that, while insulting and rather tactlessly voiced, were justified. For all she knew, he was a guy who'd taken advantage of her brother.

Would he be able to convince her otherwise?

Was he even going to try? And if he did, would she listen, or was she one of those people who, once her mind was made up, refused to change it? Skip had told him more than once about her stubbornness.

Ty had become grimly comfortable about how he dealt with his guilt. He didn't need Madeline here, stirring the pot. Mainly because he didn't know if he had it in him to come up with yet another coping mechanism.

He dumped one more bale, then got on the tractor to move to the next spot, stringing the cattle out so they had room to eat.

He drove on a few yards, then stopped when he saw a yellowish-brown mound next to the frozen creek. His rotten morning continued.

It'd been easy to blame Madeline for his bad mood and lack of concentration, but it was kind of hard to blame her for the cow lying in the willows. Ty stopped the tractor and left Alvin to keep the cows from destroying the stack of hay on the trailer.

This was one of his feistier cows, but she simply turned her head and blinked when he approached. And then he saw the dead calf. A preemie, but a big one.

"Come on, girl," he muttered, reaching out to give her a couple pats on her shoulder. She didn't react. He nudged her with his knee, carefully, since he'd had recurring problems with the joint since the accident, but again, no response.

Shit.

Ty dug under the layers of clothing he wore, pulled his cell out of his pocket and hit lucky number three with his gloved thumb. You know you're a rancher when you have the vet on speed dial.

"Hey," he said when Sam Hyatt answered. The

crackling connection told Ty the vet was in his truck, probably on the edge of the service area. "Ty Hopewell." His breath crystallized as he spoke. "Any chance you can make it up to my place this morning? I have a cow down. She's just aborted a big preemie. Calving paralysis, I'm guessing."

The best Sam could do was noon, since he was more than a hundred miles away, en route to another emergency call.

"Thanks. See you at noon." Ty ended the call, then stood for a moment studying the cow. She studied him back. Finally he shook his head and started for the tractor, where Alvin was doing his best to save the load. Ty climbed onto the seat and put the tractor in gear.

He didn't even want to think about what else might happen today.

TY WASN'T AT HOME. Madeline knocked twice. The collie hadn't barked, so it followed that Ty was out and about, doing ranch chores or some such thing.

She'd carried her cell on the walk across the wide drive, hoping to step into a service area, but no luck. If she was going to communicate with the outside world, she was going to have to travel or ask Ty if she could use his phone. He'd probably say no and then she'd end up traveling anyway.

She stood for a moment, hands on hips, debating whether to check the barn or the shop first, then caught sight of movement in the field. A tractor, slowly heading away from her. It stopped a few seconds later and

Ty got off and walked back to the load of hay, climbing on the trailer to avoid the crush of cows. The collie was snapping at the animals, fending them off.

Ty was feeding, and it looked as if he'd just begun. How long would it take to feed all those cattle? Should she wait?

The sky was darkening, the clouds hugging the top of the mountain range. The last weather report she'd accessed before leaving Reno had promised days of on-again, off-again snowstorms. If she wanted to store up on provisions, such as toilet paper—how on earth had she forgotten toilet paper?—and set up a way to get mail, she needed to take advantage of this window of opportunity. She would catch up with Ty as soon as she got back.

It was wasteful to run the generator while she was gone—Ty had said the fuel was low. So she went to the barn, covering her ears until she reached out with one hand and cautiously flipped the toggle switch he had used to start the machine. After a low drone of protest, it stilled.

The silence that followed was intense and Madeline felt an instant flood of relief.

They were definitely going to look into solar power.

THE COW LOOKED NO BETTER when Ty stopped on his way back from feeding. Four hours until Sam got there... Once again Ty tried to get her to her feet, and once again she refused to budge. It was gearing up to snow again, but at least the cold wasn't as bitter as it'd been the week before. Ty got on the tractor, feeling helpless. Losing a cow wasn't in the budget. He'd already lost a calf. He wasn't up for a double loss.

He parked the tractor in the barn, cocking his head and wondering why things didn't seem quite right. It took him a second to realize the generator wasn't running.

Shit.

He climbed off the tractor, wincing as he twisted the knee he'd been so careful of when he'd nudged the cow. Ty paused for a painful moment, resting his hands on his thighs, knowing from experience that if he waited a few seconds, let his knee recover, there would be no lasting damage. He took a cautious step once the pain subsided, and the knee held. Good. One point for him—his first today. But if the generator engine had seized... It hadn't. The engine was cool to the touch. The oil level was fine. The collar of wires appeared to be all right. No short. And Madeline wasn't there in the barn, demanding to know what had happened to her power.

Ty scratched his head, then reached out to flip the switch. The machine started. Ty turned it back off. Madeline had turned off the power? That seemed odd. Granted, she seemed a bit odd herself, but still...

Ty didn't want to initiate contact. Even though he'd come to the conclusion that the smartest thing he could do was to cooperate, the logic part of his brain hadn't quite conquered the pissed-off part. It turned out, though, that he didn't need to worry about initiating contact. Her car was gone.

For good?

He doubted it, but he climbed the porch steps to check if her belongings were still there. That plan was squashed when the knob refused to turn in his hand.

Madeline had locked her door.

CHAPTER FIVE

THE DRIVE DOWN THE mountain was more difficult than the trip up had been yesterday, giving Madeline no time to dwell on either the ranch or Dr. Jensen. The ruts in the snow had frozen overnight and kept unexpectedly catching her tires, yanking the car to the side of the road and the snowbanks there. But as she had told Ty, Madeline was no rookie at driving in the snow. Her grandmother, after retiring from her teaching job, had lived at the end of a particularly nasty road in northern Maine, close to where she had grown up.

After a few close calls—closer than Madeline was entirely comfortable with, since she didn't want to hike back up the mountain and ask Ty to pull her out of the ditch—she arrived at Barlow Ridge. Unable to wait any longer, she stopped at a crossroad and dialed Connor's number. He didn't answer, even though it was close to noon back home.

Madeline stared at the phone. Connor always answered. His phone was practically embedded in his palm. Was he not answering on purpose? Was this his way of not enabling her obsession over the investigation?

She tried again, then fired off a text.

I want to talk about the ranch. Pick up.

Nothing.

Madeline ground her teeth, then shoved the phone into her pocket and pulled the car back out onto the road. She drove from snowy gravel onto cleared pavement as she passed the first houses.

The town was tiny, and while there were many communities this size scattered throughout the northeast, the sheer isolation of this one made it seem even smaller. Madeline estimated the population at less than five hundred. She had to estimate, since for some reason towns in Nevada didn't boast population—they announced altitude. So while she was happy to know that the reason she couldn't breathe was because she was at 5,160 feet above sea level, from an anthropological point of view, population was a much more interesting statistic.

Fields and ranches bordered the paved streets until she reached the nucleus, which consisted of a mercantile, a bar, a post office, a school and a prefab metal building that appeared to be the community center. At the far end of town, on the road leading to civilization, was another metal building, red. Perhaps a fire station?

Madeline parked in front of the mercantile, which had an honest to goodness hitching post in front, festooned with garlands and red ribbons. Sleigh bells hung on the door, jingling merrily as she let herself into the store, which seemed to be deserted. Madeline didn't mind. She stood for a moment, studying the wild variety of merchandise crammed into too small a space.

Holy smoke. Where did she begin? The aisle with

the small artificial Christmas tree, or the one with the saddle?

Madeline pulled her list out of her jacket pocket and unfolded it. It appeared that whatever she could possibly want—a jar of mustard or a bag of hog chow—was here. She picked up a plastic basket, since there were no carts, and slowly started down the first aisle, cataloging what was where, since she'd a feeling she would be back.

"Can I help you?"

Madeline nearly jumped out of her skin at the accusing growl from behind her. She whirled and saw a small gray-haired woman at the counter. She hadn't been there a few minutes ago. Where had she been? Crouching down, maybe?

Madeline automatically moistened her lips as the woman glared at her. "I just needed a few things. You are open, aren't you? The door was unlocked so I assumed—"

"I'm open," the woman said flatly. "Where'd you come from?"

"New York. A little town near—"

"Here."

Madeline cocked her head. "Excuse me?"

"Since this town is at the end of the road, you aren't traveling through. Where are you staying while you're *here?*"

"Oh." Madeline forced the corners of her mouth up even though she didn't feel at all like smiling at this crabby woman. "I'm half owner of..." Damn. Why didn't the place have a name? "...that ranch up Lone Sum Road."

"Lonesome Road?" the woman asked with a mystified expression. "You mean Lone *Summit* Road?"

"Uh, yes," Madeline said stiffly. "That's exactly what I mean. Ty Hopewell is my partner. Actually, he was my brother's partner, but my brother passed away."

"You're Skip's sister?"

"Yes."

"I'll be." She shook her head again, frowning at Madeline as if she were a particularly nasty specimen.

"Why?" Madeline made no further attempt at politeness. She wanted an answer. Why was it so incredible that she was Skip's sister?

"Skip was laid-back. Not an uptight bone in his body." The woman's eyes traveled over Madeline in a way that made her back stiffen. Okay, maybe she was wearing her black pants rather than jeans, but she was saving the jeans to clean in, since without a washer and dryer she had no clothing to spare. And perhaps a tastefully belted, knee-length navy blue wool coat wasn't the norm in extremely rural Nevada, but it didn't cry out uptight... unless it revealed a prim white blouse collar beneath it. She should have worn her red sweater.

"Yes. My brother was quite a relaxed individual." She held up the list. "Would it be all right if I continued to shop?" The woman's response shouldn't have stung. Skip had always charmed people, whereas she'd had to resort to dazzling them with logic or impressing them with her academic prowess. The shopkeeper didn't look as if she would be wowed by either. She made a dismissive gesture and Madeline walked down the nearest aisle with slow, deliberate steps. She would not be intimidated. But if this woman was representative of the local population, she wouldn't be spending too much time in town, either.

Madeline eventually stacked three loaded baskets on the counter, along with a broom, a mop and two bottles of cleaning solution. She'd be returning a full bottle to Ty.

She'd eventually found everything on her list, with no help from the retailer, who'd sat silently behind her counter as Madeline shopped. It had taken a while to find ketchup that wasn't laced with hot sauce, and the only wine she could find was red with a homemade label, which seemed to indicate that it, too, was home-made. She didn't think it was legal to sell home brew to the general public, but figured it wouldn't be for sale if it was a health hazard, so what the heck? Wine helped on those nights when she suffered from insomnia, and given her situation, she may be facing some of those nights in the near future.

"By the way, I'm Madeline Blaine," she said as the woman started ringing up her purchases.

"Anne McKirk," the woman snapped.

"…McKirk is an unusual name. I've never heard it before."

"Short for McErquiaga."

"Basque?" Madeline guessed.

"Bingo," Anne replied as she waved at the canned goods she'd rung up. "We load our own bags here."

"Oh." Madeline shook out a large paper bag and started loading. "Are there many Basque here?"

"Hmm."

Possibly an affirmative. Madeline had never met a person of Basque descent before. Fascinating culture, though.

After paying for her groceries, she tried one more time to be friendly, primarily because the mercantile was the only game in town. "I'm impressed with the wide array of merchandise you have here."

"I do try to keep an array," the woman agreed sourly. She handed Madeline her change, then stepped out from behind the counter and headed for the back of the store without another word. Madeline watched her go.

Tough crowd.

A few minutes later, Madeline stepped inside the post office cautiously. But unlike Anne McKirk, the postmistress beamed when she saw a new face cross the threshold. A Christmas wreath pin blinked on the woman's green sweater as she opened the gate separating the business area from the lobby.

"Hi," Madeline said, taking advantage of the first sign of friendliness she'd encountered since arriving in the eastern part of Nevada. "I'm Madeline Blaine, Ty Hopewell's ranching partner." It sounded ridiculous coming from her lips, but it was the truth. She was a partner and their business was ranching.

"You must be Skip's sister. I'm so very sorry about

your loss." The woman instantly closed the distance between them and enveloped her in a hug.

"Uh, yes. Thank you." Madeline wasn't a big hugger, except with close friends and family under highly emotional circumstances, but she appreciated the sentiment behind the gesture.

"We all liked Skip very much." She ran a quick eye over Madeline, making her once again aware how out of place her teaching clothes were and how little she resembled her brother, both physically and psychologically. But this lady didn't seem to find as much fault with her as Anne McKirk.

"Thank you," Madeline repeated. "How would I go about getting mail while I'm here. I'll probably only be here a matter of weeks, so if I could rent a box for a month—"

"Oh, good heavens, no."

"Uh…"

"All the boxes are rented. You simply have your mail sent here to general delivery and I'll make sure you get it. If you leave your phone number, I'll give you a call whenever you get something."

Wow. Talk about service. Only one small problem. "My phone doesn't work at the ranch."

"Do you have an iPhone?" the postmistress guessed. "You must, because that service provider isn't available in this area. If it was, I'd have one of those phones in a heartbeat."

"Yes, they are nice," Madeline agreed. *Just not around here.*

"I'll call Ty if you get mail."

"Thanks," Madeline said, realizing this was her only option. It wouldn't kill Ty to let her know if she had mail, and she didn't foresee getting any. All she was doing was covering her bases, just in case Everett needed to send legal documents or something related to the case.

"So, how is Ty doing?" There was obvious concern in the postmistress's voice.

"Umm, he seems…" Cranky? Off-putting? Madeline shrugged helplessly, hoping it was answer enough. The postmistress appeared satisfied.

"We've been worried about him. His dad lived in the area and Ty used to visit during the holidays while he was growing up."

"His father's a local?"

"Ty's family has a long legacy here. In fact, your ranch was one of the original Hopewell properties. I know he was happy to buy it back."

"I bet he was," Madeline said drily, tucking that information away.

"He attended community functions when he first moved here, but after the accident…well…like I said. We've been worried."

"I'll pass that along."

The postmistress's eyes widened. "Oh, no. Don't do that. We'll never see him if you do. Ty's shy, you know."

No, she didn't know. Did shy people snap at their business partners and accuse them of going for the jugular—which was a ridiculous accusation? Madeline faked a smile. "Mum's the word," she agreed.

"Thank you." The woman beamed, satisfied that her concern was still a secret. "By the way, my name is Susan. Why don't you take a look at our community bulletin board over there by the window and see if there's anything that might interest you while you're here. We're going to have our school Christmas pageant in two weeks and then there's the community Christmas party in the park. That's always a lovely event."

Madeline did peruse the board, which was neatly organized, each flyer and card carefully dated. There were items for sale—a goat that was specifically noted as being a pet goat, not an eating goat; an aluminum fishing boat that needed to be patched; a barely used dinette set that hadn't fit into the newlyweds' small trailer. A guy named Manny would clean your chimney and someone named Toni would tutor kids in math. There was a quilting club and a crafts club—new members welcome. Madeline wondered how many new members there could be in such a closed environment.

"Oh!" she exclaimed, causing Susan to look up at her. "I need to find some firewood."

The postmistress shook her head. "You'll have to go to the feed store in Wesley for that."

"I can't order and have it delivered?"

Another shake of the head. "Not unless you want to pay an arm and a leg."

An arm and a leg didn't sound like such a bad asking price for warmth.

"No one local has wood?"

Susan reached under the counter and pulled out a 4x6 card. "Let's make an ad." She passed the card and a marker to Madeline, who hesitated for only a moment before writing "Wanted: firewood. Half a cord will suffice."

As soon as she'd done so, she wished she hadn't written the word *suffice*. "I don't know Ty's phone number."

Susan smiled as she handed her an oversize, laminated paper that apparently served as the local phone book. There were approximately a hundred names in alphabetical order. Madeline wrote Ty's number on the ad.

"Shall I hang it?"

"No. I'll do that. You'd better get back up that mountain if you're going to beat the storm."

"I will. Thank you for all your help."

"Oh, Madeline…" Susan called from behind the counter. "Ty has some mail. Would you like to take it to him?"

"Sure." What else could she say? But as Madeline took the bundle, she couldn't help but wonder if she and Susan were committing a federal crime. Could mail be released to just anyone? If Susan wasn't going to tell, neither was she.

TY CHECKED THE COW TWICE before Sam finally showed up—thankfully, an hour early.

"Did you happen to see a small car in a snowbank on your way up?" he asked the vet conversationally.

"No, but there was a strange car in front of the post office. A blue Subaru."

So she'd made it to town. Would she make it back before the snow started? He hoped so. He had stuff to do, a cow to move.

He and Sam rode the tractor out to where the cow lay, and then Sam went to work examining the animal, which still gave no response.

"You're right. Calving paralysis," Sam finally said. "Do you want me to autopsy the calf?"

"Not this time." Madeline probably wouldn't want to spend the money. Besides, the calf was frozen.

Sam glanced across the field to the barn. "We'll need to get her somewhere where you can tend to her."

"Yeah," Ty said darkly. Tending to her meant either supporting her in a sling or turning her four times a day so that her weight didn't damage her nerves or lungs. Right now the challenge was getting her to the barn.

"I have a pretty sturdy gate," he said, shifting his gaze from the cow to the vet. The problem with ranching alone was that there was rarely another pair of hands when needed—that and the very real possibility of getting hurt and not being able to summon help. "I couldn't come up with a way to manhandle her onto it myself."

"*I'll* lend a hand," Sam said drily.

Ty grinned. "I appreciate it."

The two men walked back to the tractor. "So who's driving the Subaru that isn't in the snowbank?"

"My late partner's sister."

"Is she going to become an active partner?"

"Not if I can help it." Ty was surprised at the bitterness in his voice. He made a stab at damage control after Sam sent him a questioning look. "She's a college professor and doesn't exactly fit in here. Plus…she kind of knows a lot, if you get my drift."

"Yeah," Sam said. "I think I do."

They drove back to the barn and chained the heavy metal gate to the back of the tractor like a sled, then returned to the cow, where between the two of them they managed to roll the animal onto it and tow her back to the barn. Sam rode with the cow, which acted as if she were pulled through the snow on a makeshift toboggan on a regular basis.

Once the cow was in the barn, Ty and Sam got her arranged on the sling Sam had brought with him, then used the tractor bucket to lift her and attach the sling to supports on the metal rafters. Both men were breathing hard when they got done. The cow, on the other hand, seemed happy to be off the ground.

Ty had only had this happen once before, with an older cow, and she'd regained the use of her hindquarters within a matter of days after calving. That wasn't always the case, however.

"How long shall I give her?" he asked the vet.

Sam ran a hand over the stubble on his jaw. "If she's not back on her feet in two weeks, tops, then…" He gestured philosophically.

Ty nodded. This was an expensive cow.

"Let's go to the truck and I'll give you the meds. Just yell if you have any more trouble. It's been pretty slow this month, so I should be available."

"Thanks." Ty walked with Sam to his panel truck. "One more thing. If you do happen to see that little car stuck somewhere…"

Sam grinned. "You'll be the first guy I call."

CONNOR WASN'T ANSWERING his phone. Madeline closed her eyes, her shoulders sinking as she released a frustrated breath and let her head fall back against the seat rest of her car. Ninety-nine percent of the time, she maintained a high level of self-control, but right now she was edging into one-percent territory.

Right.

Who was she trying to kid? She'd been making regular sorties into one-percent territory since being relieved of her teaching duties. Probably her stupidest move was when she'd ignored Everett's advice and tried to talk to Dr. Jensen in the staff parking lot. When she'd stepped out from behind her car and into his path, her former mentor's expression had been first surprised and then cold. All he'd said was, "I can't discuss the case."

"It's not like I'm wearing a wire," Madeline had replied in as wry of a voice as she could manage, stung that the man who'd helped build her career was treating her like a leper. Surely the coldness was a facade. When Jensen shook his head and pushed past her, though, she'd known he was serious. He couldn't or wouldn't discuss the case.

Later, when she'd come to her senses, she was able to see that he'd had legal reasons for not speaking to her, perhaps even for being so cold and unemotional. But all she'd wanted was a bit of reassurance. A look, a wink, a hint that all would be well. He, of all people, knew how important her studies and her job were to her. It wouldn't have killed him to do something to ease her mind.

She tossed the phone onto the seat beside her and put her idling car into gear. No sounding board today. She was on her own—a feeling she'd become quite familiar with over the past several weeks.

CHAPTER SIX

IT WAS A FEW MINUTES after one o'clock and Madeline still wasn't back. Sam hadn't called, as he'd promised to do if he saw the blasted woman stuck somewhere, so she had to be off doing…something.

None of your business.

Ty headed out to the barn to check the cow. Dark clouds obliterated the top of Lone Summit. The snow would start falling soon. A headache started to throb near his temples.

It was a hell of a lot easier to tell himself that if she got into trouble it was none of his business than to believe it. She wouldn't be here if Skip was still alive. If Madeline Blaine got herself into trouble, it was Ty's job to get her out again. Like it or not, insulted or not, he owed it to Skip, so he felt a small surge of relief when Alvin suddenly went on alert while Ty was dragging straw bales close to the cow in preparation for bedding changes. The collie never barked at intruders, only at other animals, but there was no mistaking his message. Madeline was back.

When Ty left the barn a few minutes later, Alvin close at his heels, he found Madeline's car parked next to Skip's house, and he had to admit to being impressed.

Not many people, including her brother, could have driven that little beast up Lone Summit Road. Madeline had a talent.

A few minutes after he was back inside, she knocked on the door. He kept his expression carefully blank as he answered, determined to keep it businesslike between them, regardless of any tactless accusations that might pop out of her mouth. Madeline stood on the top porch step, looking professorial in a dressy navy wool coat, white blouse and black slacks underneath it. Her straight dark hair just brushed her shoulders from under a classic beret. The only way she could have looked more out of place would have been if she was wearing a skirt. Or maybe a swimsuit.

She held out a new bottle of 409 cleaner. "Thank you for the loan."

He took the bottle without arguing that it was a lot fuller than the one he'd lent her. "You're welcome."

One corner of her mouth tightened in an expression of uncertainty—the first he'd ever seen on her face. "I also have your mail. The postmistress suggested I bring it to you. I hope that was all right. It was hard to say no, and I was very careful not to lose any."

As if she could. There were four rubber bands holding the catalogs, newspapers and magazines into a U-shape, with the letters and cards tightly sandwiched in the middle. He could see the colorful envelopes of Christmas cards in the bundle.

"Probably just junk mail, anyway." He shifted his weight. "I think we should have a sit-down."

Her eyebrows lifted slightly. What had she thought? That he was going to spend his days dodging her? Or that he needed more time to cook the books?

"When would be a convenient for you?" she asked politely.

"How about this afternoon?" The sooner he got this over with, the better.

"How about tomorrow?" The words shot out of her mouth and this time his eyebrows rose. "I *have* to get that house cleaned." She sounded almost desperate. She may even have suppressed a shudder. Well, it wasn't his fault she was living there.

"Tomorrow then. Ten o'clock."

"Ten o'clock." She glanced past him in the general direction of his home office, formerly the dining room, where his computer screen saver was flashing a slide show of Piedmontese cattle. "If you don't mind me asking, what cellular company do you use?"

"It's local."

"It provides internet?"

"It does." Ty wondered if she'd been comparing service service packages and wanted him to switch.

"I don't get service here."

Ah. "Do you have an iPhone?"

"Yes."

"That would explain it. We don't—"

"Have that service at the ranch. I know. It seems strange to me to have areas where some services work and others don't."

"Welcome to the rural West," Ty replied drily, then

waited to see if she was angling to use his computer or phone. If so, she was going to have to come out and ask.

She didn't.

"I'll see you at ten o'clock." She took a small backward step, still holding his gaze and apparently forgetting she was at the edge of the stairs. Ty automatically reached out, but she regained her balance before he could touch her. He dropped his hand. Madeline's eyes shifted from his hand to his face, her cheeks flushing slightly.

"I'll see you tomorrow," she said in a stiff voice.

"Ten o'clock," he repeated, for want of anything better to say.

She left without another word, stalking away along the snowy path. Ty watched her go, following the motion of her hips beneath the soft wool coat before he caught himself. Not the woman to be ogling, even if she did have a nice ass. He wished he hadn't noticed, but he had.

He went back into the house and firmly closed the door. Maybe he needed a little time away from the ranch.

SCRUBBING ALWAYS HAD A therapeutic effect on Madeline. After her suspension, she'd scrubbed her apartment floors twice, and then she'd started on the walls. The difference between her apartment and this doublewide was that her apartment hadn't needed cleaning. Every surface in Skip's house turned to mud when water was applied. She washed, rinsed, washed again. Finally, after two and a half hours, she was satisfied, but not exhausted enough to take a nap, as she'd hoped.

Too much to think about, but for once it didn't involve the Jensen situation. Rather, the ranch. And Ty. She couldn't believe how fast he'd yanked his hand back after realizing she wasn't going to fall off the porch—as if he was afraid of catching something by touching her. She was surprised he hadn't thrown his shoulder out.

Madeline stowed the cleaning equipment and shook off the rubber gloves, which fell from her hands into the sink easily, since there'd been only one size available at the mercantile: extra large.

She opened her briefcase and pulled out the printed list of ranch assets. Livestock. Equipment. Land. She sipped the cup of tea she'd just brewed and read down the list, which was lengthy and must have taken Ty a long time to compile. She had no idea what half the stuff was, which was going to slow down the informal inventory she wanted to take prior to the meeting. She should have looked up pictures on the internet before coming, but she'd assumed she'd be able to access her satellite internet from the ranch. And that Ty might cooperate. She was going to have to do the best she could, since her accountant had told her to make sure everything that was supposed to be on the ranch was indeed here.

She wasn't going to count the cows right away. There were a lot of them, each worth a couple thousand dollars, since they were registered stock. Skip had owned a horse, though, which Madeline assumed was one of the three she'd noticed in a smaller field next to the cattle pasture. He'd been quite proud of Gabby, a registered quarter horse he'd planned to breed. Skip always had been a sucker for babies.

She put a small question mark on her list.

Equipment...what exactly was a swather? Another question mark.

Madeline continued down the three-page list, marking more items.

Three tractors? She'd seen only two in the barn. A large one with a cab and the not-so-large one that Ty had been driving out in the field. Question mark.

By the time she flipped over the last page she had the distinct feeling that she had a lot to learn—about farming equipment if nothing else.

No time like the present.

Madeline put on her light blue puffy coat and stocking hat, leaving her blue wool coat and beret still drying over a chair in the cold kitchen. Pushing her feet into her boots, she let herself out of the house. Fat flakes of snow drifted down from the white sky, the kind of snowflakes she and Skip had caught on their tongues when they were kids, ignoring their grandmother's warning about airborne pollutants.

Madeline missed her brother.

She stopped in the middle of the wide ranch yard, debating where to begin. There was the barn, which she'd already been in, a covered shed with equipment parked in it and three smaller buildings. The equipment shed seemed the easiest place to start, so she trudged in that direction. Ty hadn't been there recently. There was no path beaten through the snow.

Small drifts had encroached into the shed, but for the most part it was dry—except for where a hole in the roof had allowed snow to build up in a far corner. Ty had no equipment parked in the area, but he also hadn't fixed the hole. She'd been on the property for less than twenty-four hours, but she had a very strong feeling that the ranch Skip had been so proud of was something of a wreck. If Ty was pouring money into it, it didn't show.

WHAT IN THE HELL was she doing?

Ty stood in front of his sink and watched through the window as Madeline disappeared into the equipment shed. If he hadn't been mistaken, she was carrying a clipboard. Whatever she was doing, she was taking her own sweet time.

He watched for several minutes before finally reaching into the soapy water to drain the sink. But he couldn't bring himself to go back to the pasture grant he was working on. It bothered him, having someone else on the ranch he'd lived alone on for so long, and no matter how often he told himself that she owned half the equipment, the land and the cattle—for now, anyway—he couldn't shake off his urge to protect what was his. And that included his privacy.

Madeline was apparently camping in the equipment shed. What was so fascinating in there? Was she running an inventory?

Ty's fingers gripped the edge of the sink. Of course she was. She thought he was selling stuff and pocketing the money. He turned away from the window and went back to his desk, where the grant papers were arranged, yellow legal pad with his handwritten notes paper-clipped to the various sheets.

After a few minutes, he dropped his pen and leaned back in his chair. It was impossible to concentrate with Madeline out there doing who knew what.

MADELINE PUSHED HER HAIR behind her ears. Honestly? She'd thought this equipment would be easier to recognize. She'd figured out the rake, had taken her best guess at what a baler was. The swather was still a mystery.

One thing she was certain of—there was no tractor in this shed, either. Where was the third tractor? If he'd sold it, he'd done it since October, when her accountant had received the inventory list.… If Ty had ever bought it in the first place. Maybe it was in the barn.

Madeline let herself in through the side door. The inside of the barn was no warmer than outside, kind of like her trailer, but it was dry and smelled of hay. And next to the hay was a small piece of equipment with a bucket on the front that quite possibly qualified as the Kubota tractor on her list.

Yes. Kubota was spelled out on the side and she felt a twinge of guilt for suspecting Ty of wrongdoing. She'd never seen anything quite like this small machine. It was about the size of a Smart Car, with an open cab and a bunch of levers. She ran a hand over the frame, then, after a quick glance around, slid into the seat and took the wheel.

This was her kind of tractor. She'd never driven anything other than a car, but the idea of driving a piece of heavy equipment—well, maybe not so heavy in the case of this little tractor—held a novel appeal. She took hold of one of the levers, then another. The gear knobs were smooth and fit her palm perfectly. But…what did they do?

A rustling noise behind the stack of hay at the back of the barn startled her and she slid off the tractor seat.

"Ty?"

No answer, but she heard the noise again.

She walked around the hay to investigate, then stopped dead. A buff-colored cow with the most gorgeous soft brown eyes was hanging from a sling suspended from the rafters.

It took Madeline a second to realize that her mouth was open. She closed it and took a few steps forward. The cow went back to eating out of the manger in front of her.

"What happened to you?" Madeline asked softly.

The cow, of course, did not answer. She didn't seem to be in pain. The contraption that suspended her was comprised of canvas, straps and metal supports. It looked almost like a traction device that allowed her feet to just touch the floor. How long had this poor animal been hanging here? More importantly, why was she hanging here?

Madeline left the barn, still wondering what on earth had happened to that poor cow, and walked to the building at the edge of the plowed part of the yard. The wood was old and weathered to a silver color. As far as she could tell, no paint had ever touched its surface. She pulled the pin out of the hasp and opened the door, then jumped back as mice scurried across the floor. She lost her footing and fell on her butt in the wet snow.

Just as quickly she scrambled to her feet—or tried to. She slipped, went down to her knee, bruising it, then finally managed to regain her balance. She didn't stop to brush herself off, but instead slammed the door shut and slipped the pin back into place.

No inventory necessary there, since the building was stacked full of bags and bags of animal feed and grain; but even if she'd had to take a look at the contents, she wouldn't have done it until she'd purchased a large and ferocious cat. Madeline hated mice. Hated them.

The butt of her jeans was soaked through to her skin, but she forced herself to walk to the next building. *You are a Yankee. You can face adversity.* Her heart was beating faster as she undid the latch on the door, and when she opened it, she jumped back.

She really hoped Ty wasn't watching her.

No mice. Madeline cautiously stuck her head in. Saddles, bridles, horse stuff everywhere. She went inside, still on high mouse alert, and glanced down at her list.

A Capriola saddle. A Circle Y saddle. Both marked

as Ty's personal property. Skip's saddle was designated as "maker unknown."

Madeline looked at the tack, neatly stored on trees fastened to the far wall. Which one had been Skip's?

She inspected the saddle closest to her, running her hand over the leather, darkened with age or oil, she didn't know which. There was a faint stamp on the part that the stirrup was suspended from, obviously a maker's mark. She couldn't read it, so she went on to the next saddle in the line. The mark read Capriola. The next one Circle Y. The dark saddle must have been Skip's. She went back to the dark saddle, cupped her palm over the horn then lifted the saddle strings and let them fall again. Had her brother ridden well?

She let herself outside a few seconds later, the cold air moving right through her damp pants. She pressed on in spite of the chill.

One building left, the one closest to the barn. But like the shed, there was no path plowed to this one. Apparently it held nothing Ty had needed after the snow fell. It was locked.

Madeline lifted the padlock with one finger, then let it fall back against the weathered wood of the door. Interesting. What needed to be locked up on a ranch that left obviously valuable saddles unlocked?

She was still thinking about the locked shed a few minutes later as she stripped out of her wet jeans in her unheated bathroom. Probably nothing. The building was small. She'd simply wait and ask Ty about it when they met. That and the cow.

TY WAS ACTUALLY MAKING some headway on the grant when the phone rang. Cursing under his breath, he thought about not answering it, but no one called him simply to chat, so it had to be important. Even his mother wrote emails instead of phoning. He wasn't a good conversationalist.

"Ty?"

He didn't recognize the voice. "This is Ty."

"This is Susan Echeverry from the post office. Is Madeline there?"

As if.

"Uh, no." Why on earth would Susan Echeverry be calling Madeline? At his place?

"Well, if you wouldn't mind passing along a message, I found her some wood. Deirdre will sell her half a cord."

And how is she going to get her wood up to the ranch?

"I'll pass the message along."

"Did you get your mail?"

"I did," Ty answered politely, glancing at the grant forms.

"Just thought I'd check," Susan said with a small laugh.

"I got it."

She did not take the hint. Susan loved to talk. "Will Madeline be staying long? I mean, is this a permanent move?"

The thought made Ty's blood pressure spike. "I don't

think so. She's a professor of some sort. I think she has classes in January."

"So she's only here to visit? In the middle of the winter?"

"It appears so," Ty said wearily. "Uh, Susan, I have a grant I need to meet a deadline on...."

"Oh, yes. Of course. Well, I'll talk to you later, Ty."

"Goodbye, Susan."

"Don't forget to pass the message along."

Ty rolled his eyes. "I'll remember. Thanks for calling." He ended the call before Susan got going again.

Weird how he felt so mentally exhausted as he walked back to the desk. Because of Susan? Or Madeline poking through his things?

MADELINE TRIED TO WORK on the memoir after she'd returned to the house, but it was impossible to focus—probably because the temperature felt as if it was approaching the low forties. She still had her coat on and every now and then she paced the length of the room for warmth. Wood smoke came out of Ty's chimney. Was he trying to make her leave by freezing her out? She'd considered asking him for wood the night before, but had noticed, when she'd picked up the cleaning supplies, that his stove was the pellet variety. Hers was the wood-burning kind.

Madeline walked over to put her hand on the frigid surface of the stove, trying to imagine heat rolling out of it. What kind of man let his business partner freeze to death?

The kind who didn't want her anywhere near the property she owned half of.

Madeline leaned back against the stove, pressing her gloved hand to her forehead. Ty wasn't trying to freeze her out. The generator was low on fuel, and short of inviting her to stay with him, what could he do?

There. She was doing her best to keep an open mind. Truly she was, but when she'd started this journey, she'd envisioned arriving at a quaint ranch with plank fences, charming outbuildings, power she could depend on. Instead she had spotty electricity and a cold, ramshackle double-wide with outbuildings to match and a cow hanging in the barn. On top of that she had a defensive business partner she didn't know if she could trust. The information that this had once been Hopewell land bothered her. Had Skip known?

Madeline opened the freezer compartment of the refrigerator and pulled out a frozen dinner, which, judging from the amount of frost on the package, had been frozen more than once. She hoped her cheese enchiladas had not been compromised. And she wished the oven would light.

Power. She probably needed the stupid generator to heat the glow plugs that ignited the gas flame in the oven. That was the way her gas oven worked at home. Crap. What she wouldn't give for the good old-fashioned pilot light right now. Madeline was starving and she obviously wasn't going to be eating cheese enchiladas unless she sucked on them like a Popsicle. She hated this place.

Open mind. Open mind.

She yanked a box of cereal off the pantry shelf, tearing the packaging as she ripped into it. Since she did not own a bowl, only a large pack of paper plates, she ate handfuls straight out of the box. Not exactly elegant dining, but it took the edge off. When she'd told Ty to donate Skip's household items to charity, she hadn't realized that someday she might need those items. That someday she'd be at the ranch, determining why her additional source of income, the one that was going to help pay her share of her grandmother's assisted-living facility fee, was not working out as planned.

So was Ty a rotten manager? Were there extenuating circumstances other than the state of the cattle market? All the equipment seemed to be there. Or so she assumed, since the number of unidentified entries on the list roughly corresponded to the number of weird objects and pieces she was unable to identify. She could assure her accountant that Ty was not an equipment embezzler.

Now she had to figure out if the money he kept shoveling into the operation was justified, and if it was all actually going into the ranch…but how was she going to do that? This had all seemed much easier in her apartment back home.

She set the cereal box down and went to stare out the window at the barn and the snowy pasture beyond. She no more belonged here than she belonged in a chorus line. The place was a wreck. A money pit. Without Skip at the helm, directing the business end of things, it wasn't going to provide any kind of income to put toward her grandmother's care. It might even end up costing Madeline money. She could feel her open mind squeezing shut.

I am so sorry, Skip, but I don't love the ranch and I'm not wild about your friend.

CHAPTER SEVEN

TY'S HOUSE WAS WARMER than Madeline's, since his
pellet stove was pumping out heat, but in many ways
the place was almost as stark. He had more furniture,
heavy-duty leather stuff, and a few magazines lying
about, but there were no homey touches. No photos,
no mementos or bric-a-brac. Perhaps that was why the
house seemed larger on the inside than it looked from
the outside.

"Put your stuff here," he said, gesturing at the kitchen
table, where he had his laptop open and ready to go.

Madeline set down her folder of papers. She really
wanted to warm herself by the fire, but instead sat on
one of the sturdy wood chairs at the table. Ty sat opposite. He said nothing, which didn't help the tension that
had been steadily growing between them since she'd
stepped into his house. Or maybe it was only growing
in her. There was something about the way his dark
eyes were assessing her that made her want to shift in
her chair.

Madeline cleared her throat and glanced around
the room, which bore no sign of the upcoming holiday
season. Not even a Christmas card on display, and she
knew he had some, because she'd seen the envelopes in

the mail she'd delivered. "Do you visit your family for the holidays, or do they come here?" she asked, hoping to ease into more serious matters with small talk.

Ty's expression didn't change. "If I leave, I have to arrange for someone to feed, so I just stay put."

She was about to say, "So your family visits you," when she realized that wasn't what he meant. "You spend Christmas alone?"

"Yes. Any more questions?" he asked in a way that made her feel her innocent inquiry had been rude. Madeline shook her head. Ty watched her for a moment, as if ascertaining that she truly had no more questions, then he reached out and jiggled the mouse.

"I trust your inventory went well," he said conversationally as the screen came up.

"Uh, yes," Madeline said, surprised that he'd realized what she'd been doing. She wondered if he'd seen her fall on her butt after finding the mice in the grain shed.

"I have all the ranch accounts here. Where shall we begin? Your accountant has seen them, but I can answer any questions you have as we go." He glanced up at her. "Have you read through the business plan I sent him?"

She'd skimmed it, but had had other things on her mind at the time. Such as her job and the trouble there.

Madeline took a moment to compose herself. Ty slowly clenched the hand that rested on the table into a fist as he waited. He obviously knew something was up. She had to get this over with.

"The ranch is not at all what I thought it would be," she said carefully. Ty didn't respond. He was probably aware that she'd gleaned her idea of ranching from television and the movies. "I think my wisest move would be to put the place in the hands of a professional."

"Like a manager?"

"A real-estate broker. One that specializes in ranch properties. I want to sell my half of the ranch. If you want to buy my interest, of course, I would sell to you with no problem." She met his eyes, half afraid of his reaction. It was not what she expected.

"Sure," he said sarcastically. "Let me grab my checkbook."

"Ty—"

"You planned to do this all along, didn't you?" His expression remained impassive, but his voice became low and gritty as he spoke. Challenging.

Madeline sat straighter in her chair and met his gaze dead-on, refusing to be the bad guy. "I came with an open mind."

He snorted. "It seems to me that you came convinced I was cheating you."

"I wanted to see the ranch my brother bought, and to try to understand why it was no longer making money. I apologize for insulting you."

"And now you've decided to sell without seeing any part of the operation, having any of those questions answered. Well, good luck finding a buyer."

"*You* bought the place."

Ty leaned forward, his expression intense, emphasizing the sharp angles of his face, the hollows of his cheek. "Things have changed. Banks don't like loaning money on properties like this in the best of times, and in case you haven't noticed, we're not in the best of times right now."

"How did you get the initial loan for this place?" she asked, wishing she hadn't felt his warmth, caught the disconcerting scent of spicy soap when he'd leaned closer. It was distracting her.

Ty's mouth clamped shut. They both knew the answer. Skip had made a huge down payment, money she had recouped from the life insurance. Ty was still making monthly payments to her on top of his half of the mortgage. "I sold my soul," he finally said.

"What does that mean?"

He shook his head. "Go ahead and list the property. Just don't hold your breath for a quick sale."

"Obviously. This place needs a lot of work."

He looked at her, clearly stunned. "This place is fine."

Oh, he had to be kidding. "It's a disaster. Old buildings—"

"Those old buildings are sturdy and well built."

"Barbed-wire pastures."

"What do you want? Miles of white plank fences? This isn't Kentucky horse country."

"An old, ramshackle, freezing-ass-cold double-wide."

"You got me there."

Madeline shifted her jaw sideways as she studied Ty. She didn't generally speak without thinking, didn't use terms like "freezing-ass."

"There is a cow hanging from a medieval torture device in the barn," she stated.

"Calving paralysis. She can't use her hindquarters because of nerve damage."

"Why is she hanging?"

"If I don't hang her, I'd have to turn her every four to six hours. Cows get muscle damage if they lie in one position for too long."

"Turn her? Like a pancake?"

"I roll her over."

That she would like to see. How did one roll a cow? "Is this common?" Madeline asked incredulously.

"It happens every now and then, especially in older cows."

"And the prescribed treatment is to hang them," she repeated.

"Richer ranches have aqua tanks."

Madeline drew back slightly. "You don't mean a swimming pool for...cattle?"

"More like a tank. The water supports the cow's weight."

She was so not ready for this. Hanging cattle. Floating cattle. Oh, yes. Time to get out of this business. She cleared her throat and made an effort to keep her voice even as she asked, "Why are you so certain this place will take a long time to sell if it's in such grand shape? After all, you've put almost all of *our* profits back into it."

"Lack of power. Ranchers can't irrigate without power."

"You aren't irrigating."

"I...*we* are raising a small herd of specialty cattle. I swap our meadow hay, which doesn't need irrigation, for alfalfa, and bring the feed cost down. Unless some-one comes along who also wants to run a small-scale specialty operation, the power will be an issue. Most ranchers want a bigger herd than I have, and to be able to raise the hay to feed them."

"Then we need to put in some power."

"Got a million bucks? That's what the local power company wants to put electricity up the road."

"I was thinking solar power." Ty simply stared at her. "I know it's an expensive outlay to begin with, but it'll make the property more attractive, and we'll recoup the money when we sell."

Ty continued to study her, as if expecting her to suddenly come to her senses. It made her feel vaguely stupid, a feeling she did not care for one bit. "It makes sense. You could irrigate and the property will be more salable."

"You can't run a pivot, or even wheel lines, on solar."

"What's a pivot? And wheel lines?"

"A pivot is a giant sprinkler connected to a pump. On a regular power grid, it costs more than ten grand a month to run. That should give you an idea of how much power they use. You don't have the room to store that much energy on this ranch. If you did, then the hay-fields would be covered in shiny black solar-collecting rectangles and it would be a moot point."

"Skip liked you." Her rapid change of subject seemed to throw him, and she felt a sense of satisfaction. She needed to regain control of this conversation, which only emphasized to her how little she knew, how right she was to sell.

"I liked him," Ty replied cautiously. "What's your point?"

"Skip was a man who liked to please others. He wasn't a fool, but he could be led by someone who knew what they were doing."

Ty stilled. "What are you getting at?" he repeated. "That I finagled him into buying a white elephant be-cause I liked it here?"

"I understand this land was once in your family."

Ty glanced down at the table for a moment. When he looked up again his features were set in hard lines, and Madeline knew she had pushed too far, though she didn't feel as if she was pushing at all. Facts were facts.

"My great-great-grandfather was a very successful man who homesteaded in this area. He married a local girl. Most of the land in this valley was probably *in the family*," he said sarcastically. "Then things changed. Parcels were sold off during the drought years, the De-pression, the World Wars. After my father left, none of the land was in the family anymore. But—" he stabbed a finger at the table and Madeline drew back, putting distance between herself and his anger "—the bottom line is that it would have been damned hard to buy any land in this area that hadn't at one time been owned by some branch of the family. I didn't purchase for sentimental reasons or to reclaim a family dynasty. I bought because the price was right and I had a business partner who liked the place enough to help bankroll it."

"And now his heir wants to sell her half," Madeline said. The words came out sounding harsh, cold. But she did want to sell and there was no sense sugarcoating it.

"List the property."

"I will. I assume you won't do anything to sabotage the sale."

"Nothing more than breathing," he muttered. He stood, rubbed a hand over the back of his neck.

"I'm sorry," Madeline said softly. "But this is what I have to do."

"Yeah. Right. I understand." The words came out woodenly. He looked out the window at the six-inch accumulation of new snow. "The plow should be by sometime this morning."

"Meaning you want me gone?" Madeline asked flatly.

He met her gaze. There was a depth of pain in his eyes that she found disturbing.

"Meaning that little car of yours has no problem negotiating the roads if you don't feel like staying."

WELL, IT'D HAPPENED. Ty wasn't a big drinker, but every now and then whiskey made the world look better. He didn't think anything would make the world better today, but he still pulled the Jameson off the shelf and poured a splash in a jelly glass.

How long would it take Madeline to pack up and leave? How long until he had the place to himself again for however much time it took to sell? Could be weeks, could be years. He'd been sincere when he'd told her it would be difficult to find a buyer, but knowing his luck, everything would fall into place and Madeline would have the property sold by spring.

Ty sat on a kitchen chair and gently swirled the whiskey. He might have enough money left to buy a much smaller property after he paid his debt to Madeline and the bank. Loans were almost impossible to procure nowadays, but he could keep a few cattle, continue the operation on a greatly reduced scale. But it wouldn't feed him, and frankly he'd grown attached to this ranch, had come to depend on it. It helped him cope with his guilt.

It was odd that the one place he'd found solace, however temporary, was here, where he'd worked with Skip. It hadn't happened since Madeline had told him she was flying out to meet him, but there were times while he was feeding, or fixing fence, when the peace of the land seemed to permeate his soul. Times when he felt a whisper of something that felt a bit like hope.

And then it would all go to hell. Like now.

He knew better than to listen to whispers.

MADELINE OPENED THE WINE she'd bought at the mercantile and poured a dollop into a disposable plastic glass after booting up her laptop. She wasn't imbibing because of the stress of her meeting with Ty. No. She wanted to relax before she started working on the memoir.

She wasn't a bad person because she wanted to sell her half of the ranch—a ranch she'd never intended to own in the first place. She was simply doing what she had to do. It was unfortunate that it affected Ty, but that was the way it had to be.

Madeline lifted the glass, taking a sniff. She hadn't expected much of the wine, but it was surprisingly full-bodied, with interesting notes. There was cherry, or perhaps it was blackberry. A hint of lavender. And was that vanilla?

She sipped, tilted her head in silent appreciation after swallowing, then topped off the glass and started making editing notes on the last completed chapter of the memoir. Yes, definitely vanilla.

A glass and a half later Madeline realized it was getting too dark to see her work, and reached out to flick on the light. Nothing happened.

Of course, nothing.

She shoved her feet into the boots next to the chair and then grabbed her coat. Time for some of the amenities of civilization. Skip had been nuts. Camping for a few days was one thing, but every day? Even he had to tire of this mile-long walk to the barn when he wanted to use an appliance.

Ty was just leaving his own house when she opened her door. He caught sight of her and hesitated, as if he was going to reverse course, but instead he sucked it up and continued down the path to the barn, the dog at his heel. Madeline refused to be the chicken, so she did the same, even though the simple laws of physics decreed that, traveling at their given speeds, they would arrive at the barn at the same time.

As it turned out, Ty beat her by a few seconds, perhaps because her legs were not as cooperative as usual. The snow was deep.

"Surprised I'm still here?" she asked. As opposed to in her little car on her way down the mountain, like he wanted.

"Can't say that I am." Standing well back, he held the door open so she could pass through first.

"Careful not to touch me," she muttered.

"What?" he asked in a mystified voice.

She turned to him, standing on the threshold, tilting her chin up so she could meet his eyes, squinting slightly so that he was in focus. He seemed to be wavering. "Careful you don't touch me. You know." She reached out and gave his canvas-covered arm a few good pats. "Touch, touch, touch."

"Madeline?"

"Never mind." She turned and stalked over to the generator. She fully expected an explosion every time she started the machine and it must have shown in her face.

"Let me," Ty said, coming up beside her.

She held up a hand. "I can do it." She flipped the toggle with a flourish, then stepped back and put her hands over her ears. Ty took her arm and led her across the barn to the haystack, where he released her and took the requisite step back before she could warn him again about the dangers of touching.

"I'm going to go out on a limb here and guess that you picked up a bottle of wine at the mercantile."

"Indeed I did."

He poked his tongue into his cheek and nodded as if all the mysteries in the world had just been solved.

"It's not bad," Madeline added.

"One of my favorites," he agreed solemnly. "What is this about not touching you?"

"On the porch. Yesterday. When I almost lost my balance, you reached out to steady me, and then you recoiled."

"I did not...recoil."

"You did," Madeline said. "But that's all right. The circumstances between us are not the best, and considering what I have to do, I don't see them getting any better."

She paused, inhaling deeply, since she'd forgotten to breathe while she was speaking. Ty stared at her. Madeline stared back for a moment, wondering if his slightly aquiline nose was the product of Native American blood. And then, since there was really nothing else to say and he kept going out of focus, anyway, she turned and headed for the barn door on her still mildly uncooperative legs.

Ty didn't try to stop her, didn't protest that she was mistaken. She hadn't expected him to.

TY TENDED TO THE COW, trying not to think about what
had just transpired. Another unexpected similarity between Madeline and her brother. Neither could handle
good Basque wine—at least not Anne McKirk's good
Basque wine. But Amuma was a kick-ass brew. He'd
practically been raised on the stuff, and it had been a
good teenage party staple, but it could still sneak up
and wallop him.

Careful not to touch me.

Ty snorted softly as he ran a hand over the cow's
hindquarters. But upon consideration, he had to admit
she was right. He had recoiled—a word he'd never used
except when discussing a pull-start engine—but not for
the reason she seemed to think. He justifiably thought
she wouldn't want him touching her, being a suspect in
ranch fraud and all. He'd tried to give her some space.
He hadn't realized that she'd noticed or cared, although
come to think of it, she had seemed a bit put out.

Interesting.

Apparently Madeline had some vulnerabilities under
that hard shell of hers. How was she going to feel when
she sobered up and realized she'd let one show?

He hoped it bugged the hell out of her.

WHO WOULD HAVE EXPECTED the champagne effect
from a bottle of homemade red?

Not Madeline. The only wine in the world to influ-
ence her in this way was the bubbly stuff, which had
a hit-and-run effect. It hit her hard when she wasn't
expecting it, and then an hour later—although in this

case it was three hours later, almost nine o'clock—she was stone-cold sober. Only usually, since she rarely put herself in situations she couldn't control, she was not in a state of deep regret and embarrassment.

Oy. She rubbed a hand over her forehead and let out an audible groan, thankful she didn't have a worse headache than she did. She'd had only two glasses. What was in that stuff?

It was dark outside, time to turn off the generator. Ty was in his house. She could see his silhouette through his kitchen window. Now or never. He was probably going out to check the cow before bed—if he hadn't already done it while Madeline was sleeping with her head on her worktable.

She'd wasted a lot of light and fuel that evening, and, prior to that, said a few things she wished she hadn't. Nothing that wasn't true; but she hated showing weakness, and she'd stupidly let Ty know his revulsion bothered her. And, she thought stubbornly as she let herself out of the house, there was *no* other word for what he'd done, whether he admitted it or not. She knew a recoil when she saw one. She just didn't know why it had bothered her enough to have a drunken conversation about it. He didn't want to come in contact with her, the woman who was selling the ranch. Big deal.

Except she hadn't been the woman selling his ranch yesterday, and it did bother her. Illogical, but true.

TY WOKE UP SWEATING, the blankets thrown off the bed in his frantic attempts to pull Skip from the wreckage.

He drew in a shuddering breath as he realized he was in his house, in his bed, and then fell back against the pillow, heart pounding. How long had he been trying to rescue Skip? Minutes? Seconds? It felt like hours.

Alvin whimpered next to the bed and Ty reached out to reassure the dog before pulling the covers back up off the floor. Alvin had been through this with him before. It was going to be one of those days when Ty could barely drag himself through his chores. Even if he didn't consciously think about the nightmare, he felt the physical effects all day long.

This was his first nightmare in over three months. Why now?

It had to be Madeline, both reminding him of Skip and threatening his sanctuary. Double whammy.

The thought of putting the ranch on the market was eating at him, but he was in one hell of a position. Madeline pissed him off and his future was tied up in the operation, but he couldn't fight her.

He owed her a brother, and there was no way he could repay that particular debt, making the playing field even between them.

It was killing him. From the inside out.

CHAPTER EIGHT

MADELINE DRESSED carefully for her trip to town, wearing her jeans this time, so as not to stand out or look uptight, and the red sweater. She slipped into her light blue puffy coat, pulled on her gloves. It was cold in the house and the gloves felt good on her chilled fingers.

Ty hadn't turned on the generator that morning and she hadn't bothered to turn it on herself, since there was enough water in the storage tank for an ultraquick shower and to brush her teeth. Her decision to do without electricity had nothing to do with avoiding Ty.

She'd never before showered under polar conditions and had found it to be exhilarating in an odd way. That Yankee blood was finally reverting to form. Her hair had been safely pinned up and protected from the water by the heavy-duty shower cap she never traveled without— she couldn't risk her hair getting wet when she didn't have use of the flatiron. She hadn't counted on the copious amounts of steam created by a hot shower in a very cold environment. Her hair started to wave, but not to the point of curly embarrassment.

After putting on her beret, she let herself out of the house and walked directly to her car, head down. Still no Ty. No tractor in the field, no lights on in his house.

He must have overslept. She felt a sense of relief as she got into the vehicle. The embarrassment over lecturing him about touching her would fade, but what had she been thinking? She didn't let loose like that unless she was intimate with the other person. She wouldn't classify her relationship with Ty as intimate—or likely to become that way.

In fact, the thought was rather mind-boggling. What would it be like to sleep with a standoffish cowboy? Probably very one-sided, she decided with a tilt of her chin.

Anne wasn't at the mercantile when she arrived, so Madeline would be able to shop in peace. The teenage girl in her place smiled pleasantly.

"Can I help you find anything?"

"Just about everything," Madeline said, only half kidding as she once again took in the overwhelming hodgepodge of merchandise. "Actually, I only have a couple items I need to find. Batteries. Matches. And maybe a kerosene lantern?" No wine.

The girl came out from the behind the counter and led Madeline around the store, showing her where everything was. A much different shopping experience from the last one.

"How long will you being staying?" the girl asked as she rang up the items five minutes later.

"I'm not sure," Madeline said truthfully. If she found an agent she could work with, it could be a matter of days.

"If you're here for the Christmas pageant—" the girl

pointed at the poster taped to the door "—be sure to go. It's always fun."

"I'll do that."

Next stop, the post office. Susan, whose twinkling wreath pin had been replaced with Rudolph, greeted Madeline like a long-lost friend and told her that while she had no mail, Ty had some.

"I, uh, think I'll let Ty pick up his own mail."

"He has a package," Susan said, as if that piece of information would tip the scales.

"He'll probably want to pick that up himself," she said, heading for the door. She was not involving herself in Ty's personal business again.

"Have you arranged to have your wood delivered while the roads are plowed?" Susan called before the door closed. "It's supposed to snow again soon."

Madeline turned and marched back into the lobby. "What wood?"

"Oh," Susan said in confusion. "Didn't Ty give you the message? Deirdre Landau will sell you half a cord."

Madeline smiled tightly. "It must have slipped his mind. I'll ask him about it."

"Better hurry. It's supposed to snow again tomorrow."

Madeline crossed the street to the café in search of a satellite signal for her laptop, grumbling under her breath. Oh, yeah. She'd definitely be asking him about the wood. Meddling with her warmth trumped personal embarrassment.

THERE WAS NO PUBLIC WI-FI in Barlow Ridge, so unless she wanted to steal someone's private connection, she wasn't going to be researching real-estate agents online. Madeline drowned her disappointment in a cup of coffee at the café and a piece of excellent pie, then went to the counter and asked the waitress if she could borrow a phone book.

Back at the table, she flipped through the real-estate-agent listings. There were only a couple for the closest town, Wesley, and of those, one specialized in ranch sales. Madeline jotted down the number, wondering how this was all going to play out. She had to find someone she could trust. Someone who wasn't an old friend or acquaintance of Ty. Someone who'd look after *her* interests first and foremost. What were the odds in a rural community?

The waitress, wearing jeans and a winter sweater, came by and topped off her coffee after the other two patrons had left. "Find what you're looking for?" she asked as she sloshed coffee into the cup, somehow pouring it to the brim with a flip of her wrist without getting any on the tablecloth.

"I hope," Madeline said with a noncommittal smile. The waitress hesitated for a second, as if waiting for more of an answer. When Madeline lifted her fork and took a bite of pie, the girl gave up and carried the coffeepot back to the burner without any new tidbits of gossip.

As soon as she stepped behind the counter, Madeline reached for her phone. First, the ranch real-estate agent.

Myron Crenshaw answered the call himself and was quite happy to make an appointment. Almost too happy. Well, the market was slow, so she understood. Next she called home.

Her grandmother's phone rang through to the retirement-complex operator after ten rings—a safety precaution that Madeline appreciated. If her grandmother was unable to come to the phone, be it from illness or a fall, she wouldn't have to wait for the evening residence check before help arrived.

"Eileen is out for lunch and Christmas shopping," the manager told Madeline a few minutes later. "Connor and your cousin Jeffrey picked her up about an hour ago. She should be home around three this afternoon if you want to call back."

"Thanks." Madeline probably wouldn't drive back down the mountain today to do that; as it was, she was hoping she could get back to the ranch. Her grandmother had a cell phone, but wouldn't turn it on in public. Rude behavior, she'd said more than once. There was no need for an individual to be constantly in contact with every other person in the world. Her grandmother would love the ranch. Madeline hadn't been this out of contact in years.

No message from Connor or her lawyer, so she did something she probably wouldn't have done a few days ago. She dropped her phone into her pocket without calling for reassurance that nothing unexpected had happened. Her grandmother wouldn't want Connor taking calls if he was with her, and Everett didn't want her bugging him about the case. He had other clients, as he had gently pointed out before her flight to Nevada, and if he had updates, he'd be in touch.

She picked up the coffee cup and sipped, her gaze focused on the cheery country wallpaper on the wall opposite. Right now she had other issues to tend to, Ty's failure to tell her about the wood at the top of the list. In a way, she was glad he hadn't told her. Now she had a mission and she felt more like herself—in control and ready for action.

Ty WAS JUST DISAPPEARING into the barn when Madeline drove up to the gate. She went through the entire opening and closing procedure, getting snow in the top of her boots in the process, then ignored her groceries and marched straight to the barn after parking the car.

As she expected, Ty was with the cow, and even though it was late in the day, he didn't look as if he'd slept very well. There were shadows under his eyes, and rough stubble on his jaw, giving him a worn yet sensual look that stirred something within her—something she firmly squelched. She could have showered in a warm bathroom this morning had it not been for him.

"Why didn't you tell me about the wood?" she demanded, stopping a few feet away.

An odd expression crossed his face as he slowly lowered the water bucket he'd been about to empty into the cow's water trough, an expression that looked a lot like guilt. "To tell you the truth, it slipped my mind."

Madeline was outraged, but she kept her tone even

when she said, "It slipped your mind while I froze my butt off."

"It isn't like I twisted your arm to come here in the first place, Madeline." He lifted the bucket and poured the water, splashing some on the front of his jacket. "How long will you be staying, anyway, now that you've made the decision to sell? I mean, will you even need wood?"

"My return flight is three days before Christmas, so, yes, I need wood."

He frowned, unaffected by her gritty tone of voice, as he grabbed the pitchfork. "You can't get an earlier flight out?"

Madeline shoved her hands into her pockets. "No."

"Why are you here for so long, anyway? Don't you have classes to teach or something? I mean…" his eyes narrowed "…I went to college and I don't remember school ending at Thanksgiving."

To her horror, Madeline felt her color start to rise. "I'm on sabbatical." The words came out too fast.

Ty lifted his eyebrows. "Really." His sarcastic tone let Madeline know just what a bad liar she was. But she wouldn't talk about her…situation…with this guy. She'd already discussed recoiling yesterday, much to her regret, and that was as personal as she was going to get.

Madeline held his eyes, daring him to call her untruthful. "Really," she echoed flatly before firmly changing the subject. "I'm going to see the real-estate agent day after tomorrow. One of them, anyway."

"How many do you have lined up?" He started loading soiled straw into the wheelbarrow.

"One for now. I'll need some information from you before I meet with him."

"Not if you're using Myron Crenshaw. He sold the place to me."

She didn't ask how he knew it was Myron. The guy appeared to be the only game in town.

"Well, if I need information later, I assume I will not have to squeeze it out of you."

"Nope. I'll be the picture of cooperation," he assured her coldly. "And I'll call about the wood today." He dumped the last fork of dirty straw into the wheelbarrow. "I don't want you to freeze your ass off while you're here."

He held her gaze for what couldn't have been more than a second, although it felt like an eternity, then looked down again to pop the hay strings with three swift swipes of his knife.

Madeline took the hint and left.

TY PULLED THE PITCHFORK back out of the straw and finished spreading the bedding for the cow, his movements automatic. Things were not going well with his business partner and he hated the sharp emotions that were breaking through the numbness he worked so hard to achieve. His shield against guilt.

He leaned on the fork and stared blankly at the far wall of the barn. Madeline had every right to be here. Hell, she had a right to fling her accusations. But before she came and started stirring things up, he'd had a system to help him get through each day, one step at a time. The days may not have been rich and full, but there were good moments, and more than that, his system worked. If he didn't think, didn't feel too much, then he could make it.

Madeline was upsetting the status quo and he didn't know what to do about it other than to keep his distance. After the way she'd huffed out of the barn, stopping only to turn on the generator, he probably wouldn't have much trouble doing that.

Once the bedding was done, he shoved the pitchfork back into the nearest bale and headed toward the door, thinking he may have another nightmare in his future.

MADELINE SPENT THE afternoon stewing and working on the memoir, without much success. With the memoir part, anyway. She leaned back in her chair, taking a break and staring out the window at the snowy landscape before diving in again with renewed determination.

In six weeks everything would be sorted out, not up in the air, a state she abhorred. The ranch would be listed; her job would be safe. Ty, who had appeared from the equipment shed and started walking to his house, would be a distant memory.

With his hands deep in his pockets, his chin down and the black cowboy hat pulled low over his eyes, he gave the impression of a man who was walling himself off from the world. The collie, his perpetual shadow, tagged a few feet behind, shooting a quick look through the window at Madeline, as though sensing her gaze. Ty continued on, his loose-limbed walk rather mesmerizing.

She had to admit, from a detached point of view, he was something. If she didn't have to deal with him, if all she had to do was stare at him, Madeline had to admit that she could find a certain amount of pleasure in that. Unfortunately, she did have to deal with him, and it wasn't as easy as she had first supposed it would be.

He made her feel edgy and uncomfortable. She didn't quite know how to handle that…. She'd never felt that way before.

AFTER AN HOUR SPENT working on the grant he probably wouldn't need because he wouldn't own a ranch, Ty poured a couple fingers of Jameson and sat down at the computer. Madeline had lied to him about her sabbatical. Either that or she turned pink during normal conversation, and he had yet to see that reaction in any of their other discussions.

Once the internet was up, thanks to an expensive but remarkably quick satellite connection, he typed Madeline's name into a search engine.

There were a lot of Madeline Blaines.

He added *Dr.* before her name and *anthropology* after it.

Bingo.

Ty sipped the whiskey as he skimmed the first three articles that popped up. He'd had a feeling something was up with his business partner, and sure enough, according to the news sources, Dr. Madeline Blaine, Skip's perfect sister, was under academic investigation for suspicion of falsifying data and using blood samples without permission in an anthropological study. She wasn't the main suspect, but had worked closely with the professor accused of using blood samples intended for medical research for a different kind of study—one the donors had not agreed to.

Ty leaned back in his chair, contemplating the screen, almost forgetting that his knee was killing him after wrestling with the hay that morning. This was a most interesting turn of events. Not that it affected him one way or another in the long run. She would undoubtedly put the ranch on the market, and he wasn't going to try to talk her out of it. He'd lost that right when he'd insisted on driving when he was too damned tired to stay awake. He did, however, rather appreciate the knowledge that he was dealing with a case of the pot calling the kettle black. The only difference was that he wasn't guilty of the crimes she'd accused him of.

Was *she* guilty?

Ty turned off the computer and sat in silence, holding the half-empty whiskey glass. The sister Skip had described wouldn't have broken academic standards, but maybe there was more to Madeline than people knew.

Damn, after seeing her drunk, he kind of wondered if there was more to her than *she* knew. If she'd been anyone else, he might have been curious enough to test the waters and find out.

A small part of him was disappointed that she wasn't. Someone else, that is. The sooner she left for the East Coast, the sooner he could get his life, such as it was, back in strict order again. Then maybe he could start to feel a measure of peace once again.

MADELINE BRUSHED her teeth by flashlight that night, thinking she should have done that before turning off the power. There was a learning curve to this lifestyle. A few minutes later she made her way through the dark house, then snuggled deep into the sleeping bag on the sofa, after setting the flashlight on the floor. And there she lay for a good hour, sorting thoughts, trying vainly to fall asleep.

The image of Ty walking across the ranch yard, hands in his pockets, hat brim tilted down, kept crowding into her brain. A man who needed to be alone.

If he and Skip had been friends and partners, he couldn't have always been that solitary. He had to have had a strong bond with her brother, although Skip did sometimes tend to befriend the friendless. Did he also befriend the dishonest?

Madeline's instinct was telling her that Ty wasn't dishonest, that there were other reasons the ranch hadn't been making money. Reasons she didn't have the inclination to sift through. She wouldn't be able to fix them anyway—she didn't have the expertise, or the funds to hire a manager—so what was the point?

She was doing the right thing selling the ranch. Tomorrow she'd go to town and find a place with Wi-Fi to research real estate—

A rustling on the end table near her head cut the thought short. Madeline froze. When she heard the sound again, she identified the source. The cereal box.

Cereal boxes didn't make noises…but mice inside them did.

The scream tore from her throat as she tried to fight her way out of the sleeping bag. Something shot across her, tiny little feet pattering over her arm.

She screamed again as she fell to the floor with a heavy hip-bruising thud. Somehow she struggled free of the nylon and snatched the flashlight off the floor next to the sofa, snapping it on and waving the light in a sweeping motion. Trying to find the nasty little vermin that had helped itself to her dinner. Before it could attack again.

THE SCREAM, distorted by distance, brought Ty bolt upright in his bed.

Alvin poked Ty with his nose.

"Yeah, I heard it," he muttered to the dog as he got out of bed and felt around for his jeans. He shoved his feet in his barn boots, jogged through the house, feeling his sore knee give a pulse of pain as he rounded the corner to the kitchen. He grabbed his jacket off the hook next to the back door and slipped into it as he let himself out of the house and into the cold. He hadn't bothered with a shirt.

His heart beat faster as he jogged the distance between their houses, haphazardly buttoning his jacket with one hand as he ran. The full moon reflected off the snow, making the flashlight he carried unnecessary, but her trailer would be dark inside.

Things had been so much simpler when the only noises in the night were coyotes and the occasional owl. A light beam swept wildly through the house, reflecting off the windows and then disappearing, only to reappear again seconds later.

What the hell?

He tromped up the steps and had his hand poised to knock on the door when Madeline yanked it open and stumbled out. She did not fall into his arms, damsel-in-distress style, but instead jumped behind him, putting his body between her and…whatever.

"It's a mouse," she muttered from behind him. The light in her hand was shaking.

"A mouse."

"It ran over my arm." She was close enough that he felt the involuntary shudder that followed her words.

Okay. He was man enough to admit that would creep him out, too. Especially in the dark. When there could be a dozen of them. He took a step away from her. Either the moonlight or sheer terror gave her face an unnaturally pale cast.

"How the hell did it get in?" he said, more to himself than to Madeline. He'd caulked every crack and seam and had stuffed steel wool around all the pipe openings. It had worked for two years. Why…?

He glanced over his shoulder at Madeline, who had her arms wrapped tightly around her, probably as much from terror as from cold. All she was wearing was a long men's pajama top and thick wool socks. "Did you leave the door open?" Crazy idea, because why would anyone leave a door open in the middle of winter?

She automatically opened her mouth to protest, then shut it again.

"You left the door open."

"When I carried the stuff in from my car."

"How long did you leave it open?"

She shrugged, her arms still around her middle, which had an interesting effect on her breasts under the flannel of the pajama top. Ty forced himself to focus on her face and ignore the fact that a few too many of her buttons were undone. It was surprisingly difficult not to take that second look. "Five minutes maybe."

"In the winter?"

Her eyes snapped up to his. "What would it matter?" She ground the words out. "It's as cold inside the trailer as out. I'm amazed the pipes don't freeze."

"They're well insulated," Ty automatically replied.

She pressed her lips together. "What are you going to do about the mouse?"

"I didn't let the mouse in."

"I *cannot* sleep in there."

And he didn't want her in his place. He was having enough trouble sleeping as it was. "If I catch the mouse, then will you sleep in there?"

"I don't know," she said huskily.

Ty motioned to the open trailer door. "Get the mouse, Alvin."

The collie shot into the trailer and Ty closed the door.

"It's too dark for him to see," Madeline muttered.

"He can hear and he can smell."

Madeline shivered. Had she been anyone else, he might have put an arm around her to warm her, but he wasn't going there. Not with Madeline. Not when he was noticing her breasts.

Inside the trailer Alvin was scrambling around, his nails scrabbling on the linoleum as he zeroed in on his target. Alvin was the best mouser Ty had ever owned, including the giant Norwegian forest cat that even the coyotes hadn't bothered. There was a mighty clatter, followed by the snapping of jaws and then everything went quiet.

Ty waited a few seconds, then opened the door. Alvin came out, delicately carrying the limp mouse by its tail. He trotted down the stairs and dropped the rodent in the snow, staring at it.

Madeline made a face, then glanced back up at Ty. "How do I know that's the only one?"

"Alvin wouldn't have stopped hunting if it wasn't."

Madeline eyed the open door, her hands moving higher on her upper arms as she contemplated going inside, but she didn't move.

Ty sucked it up. "You can either sleep at my place on the sofa, or Alvin can stay here with you."

She looked as torn as he felt.

"Is it really colder in your house than it is outside?" he asked. He'd figured that the heat in the morning and evening would be enough, since the place was well insulated. Otherwise he would have seen about the wood himself. He wasn't going to let Madeline freeze to death.

"It seems like it when the power isn't on. I only left the door open a crack, so I could nudge it open with my toe. I never dreamed a mouse would be lying in wait."

"A crack is all it takes."

Madeline shuddered again and he jerked his head in the direction of his house. "Come on." He'd see that the wood was there by tomorrow, and she could spend tonight on his couch.

She shook her head. "I'll stay here. *With* the dog."

CHAPTER NINE

"ARE YOU SURE YOU WANT to stay here?" Ty asked.

Madeline was sure. She'd sleep in her car if she had to—the same car he'd told her to leave in. For two days she had stared jealously across the snowy expanse that separated Ty's warmer, cleaner, furnished, internet-equipped house from hers, but after their meetings in his house and in the barn, she wasn't going to encroach on his territory. She had her pride, even if indulging in Anne's wine had chipped away some of it.

Madeline thought of her great-grandmother—the odds she'd beaten, the hardships she'd endured. Eileen's mother, the subject of the book Madeline was working on, wouldn't have sought refuge in the house of a man she didn't understand and wasn't sure she respected—a man who made it no secret that he didn't particularly like her. She would have sooner let mice run up and down her arms, and Madeline would do the same—even if the mental picture made her feel slightly ill.

Ty frowned. "Are you all right?"

"Rodent flashback," she replied in a low voice. "Other than that, I'm fine and I'm cold. I'm going inside. Thank you for loaning me your dog." Who was now glaring suspiciously at her.

She stepped inside the trailer. The dog stayed next to Ty and pressed his head against the man's pant leg.

"Go with her," Ty said to the collie, who stared up at him with big eyes.

"Go on." Ty gestured to the door, and the collie slunk into the trailer, glancing over his shoulder as he crossed the threshold. Madeline was about to thank Ty when her gaze drifted down to his chest, illuminated in the beam of her flashlight. Where his jacket gaped open a fascinating smattering of dark hair covered an expanse of bare skin. He wasn't wearing a shirt.

She met his eyes and was surprised to see him shift self-consciously. He'd noticed that she'd noticed. It was no big deal, but somehow... "Good night." She quickly shut the door as he turned to leave, and leaned against it. What a night.

The dog padded over to the sofa and lay down, sensing that this was his post. Madeline shook out her sleeping bag—just in case—then slid back inside in short jerky motions, certain that at any moment her toes were going to encounter a squirming fur ball. But she would make it through the night without taking advantage of Ty's grudging hospitality. If she had gone to his house, she wouldn't have slept, anyway.

She preferred to spend her sleepless nights in her own territory.

A WARM WIND WAS BLOWING when Madeline opened the trailer door at five-thirty the next morning to release

Alvin from purgatory. The collie shot out and raced for Ty's house.

She stifled a yawn. Having the dog had helped her make it through the night, since he obviously hated mice, but it had taken a long time to relax enough to nod off. Then, after falling asleep, she would jerk back awake, thinking she heard or felt a mouse. Not exactly a restful way to spend the night, and if she didn't get some coffee brewed soon, she was going to eat the crystals straight out of the jar.

Madeline put the kettle on and sank into the kitchen chair, wrapping her blue wool coat snuggly around her as she waited for Ty and the heat—if he was going to turn it on for her this morning. He hadn't yesterday. She would wait, see what happened.

It occurred to her that she had no breakfast, for obvious reasons. At that very moment the tainted cereal box was on her porch, likely being devoured by mice. She shuddered. She'd have to get some tongs and take that box to the trash barrels. She was tempted to swallow her pride and ask Ty to do it for her…but she wouldn't.

The lights flickered on and Madeline glanced out the window. She'd missed Ty walking by, which rarely happened. The ranch was like an island with them the only two people on it. They were attuned to the each other's movements, the better to avoid contact. Madeline liked to think that she met adversity head-on, but there was something about this situation, living alone with Ty, that was causing her to reconsider her approach.

It would be a relief to get off the island for a few

hours today. Maybe the drive would help her gain much-needed perspective.

After the water boiled and she'd brewed a thermos full of coffee so she'd have extra for the drive to town, she headed for the shower, taking her time. She didn't have to leave for another hour.

She'd just won the battle of the flatiron, and was sipping her second cup of coffee, when Ty returned from feeding.

He drove the tractor into the barn and Madeline checked her watch. Seven o'clock on the nose. Three hours until her appointment with the real-estate agent in Wesley. She'd purposely given the man no details, preferring to lay out the situation in person while she got a read on him.

Ty came out of the barn and rolled the big barn doors shut.

Come on, Ty. I have to leave.

Madeline didn't want to go to her car until he was done feeding the animals in the pen nearest to where she was parked. She had deduced, from the very obvious physical evidence, that those animals were bulls, and he fed them by throwing hay into a manger every morning and evening. Apparently they could be kept together without fighting, and it was equally apparent that Ty did not want them mingling with the lady cows. Not yet, anyway.

Madeline drummed her fingers on the table as he followed the shoveled path to the small, tarp-covered stack of hay next to the pen. Maybe she would just suck it up and go to her car. He probably wouldn't say a word to her, anyway. About the mouse. About the possibility that she'd flashed him... It seemed he wasn't the only one to have bare-chest issues last night, but she hadn't discovered that until several hours after he'd left when she'd gotten out of bed for a nervous trip to the bathroom.

Her cheeks warmed even though she'd convinced herself several times that morning that her pajama buttons *had* been done up when he was on her porch. She would have felt the cold if they hadn't been.

She hoped.

What a night.

Ty gathered an armload of hay—almost a quarter of a bale—and trudged through the snow. After his third trip, and just as she was speculating as to whether he ever got tired of the daily routine of feeding, Ty suddenly went down, falling hard on his side in the snow. Hay scattered around him. Madeline jumped to her feet.

The collie was instantly at Ty's side, poking at him with his nose. Ty tried to stand, but his knee buckled and down he went again.

Okay, it wasn't a heart attack or seizure. It was his knee. She'd noticed him limping earlier that day as he walked past her trailer from the barn to the house.

So what now?

If she wasn't at the ranch, and he definitely didn't want her there, this was a situation he'd have to deal with on his own. And if she was the coldhearted bitch he seemed to think she was, she would let him handle it alone.

But, fortunately for him, Madeline wasn't the kind of person who could let someone suffer. Even if she kind of wanted to.

TY ALMOST HAD HIS GOOD leg under him when he heard Madeline's trailer door open and close. He looked up just as his foot slipped on the ice beneath the snow again, and he tumbled down. Crap. He was soaking wet and he really wanted her to go back inside and mind her own business.

A few seconds later she stopped in front of him and held out a hand. She wasn't wearing a coat, but she hadn't been in any hurry to cross from her porch to where he lay struggling, next to the hay. Probably enjoying the show.

He put his hand into hers, felt the surprising firmness of her grip through his glove. She planted her weight and he struggled to a standing position, balancing on one foot. "I can handle it from here," he said gruffly. "Thanks."

But Madeline refused to be dismissed. "Why don't I just help you back to your house?" He opened his mouth, but she spoke before he could. "Listen, as entertaining as it is watching you roll around in the snow, I have an appointment, and you'd better take advantage of my offer now. It's icy under the snow. You'll never make it."

True, but he hated to admit it. "Once I get my knee brace I'll be fine."

"Oh, yeah. Right as rain. I can see that," Madeline said as she slipped under his arm and took firm hold of the back of his jacket. "It won't kill you to accept some help. Consider it payback for last night."

It might not kill him, but it was going to knock his pride around. She wasn't going to take no for an answer, though, probably because it *was* payback for the night before, so he gave in and took a limping step forward with her support. Fortunately, Madeline didn't buckle under his weight.

"Does this happen often?" she asked in a conversational tone through gritted teeth, obviously making an effort not to show how heavy he was as he took another step and then another.

"Twice since the accident."

"Is this a residual injury?" Their eyes met in a way that made him extremely aware of how close she was.

"Yeah." His only real injury. When he'd been thrown clear, he'd hit his head and twisted his knee. That was it. Maybe this was his penance, having Skip's sister here, haunting him.

When they reached the porch, he removed his arm from her shoulder as soon as he was able, wanting to break a contact that had felt more intimate than it should have. He balanced on his good leg. "Thanks."

Madeline's gaze was not particularly warm or friendly, which made it easier to brush aside whatever it was he'd been feeling.

"I appreciate it," he muttered as he opened the door.

Alvin preceded him inside. Madeline stayed where she was.

"I'm leaving for Wesley in a few minutes to see the real-estate agent. If you need anything for your knee, I'd be happy to get it."

"No, thanks," he said in a clipped voice. She'd done enough. More than enough.

"Can you make it into the house all right?"

"Yeah. I'm good." But she still didn't leave. She pushed her hands into her pockets.

"Since we're even now, on the rescue front, I want to ask you a question."

He eyed her suspiciously. "Yeah?"

"If you have nothing to hide, and I'm not saying you do," she added, holding up her palms in a placating gesture, "then why do you hate having me here so much?"

"I never said I hated having you here."

Her eyes narrowed. "But I'm getting the message in so many ways. Like now."

That set him off. "What the hell do you expect, Maddie? You came here slinging accusations. No hello or anything, just 'I'm here to find out how you're screwing me over.'"

Madeline's back stiffened. "Don't call me Maddie. And yes, I had questions. Reasonable ones."

"And I've given my answers." He hopped on his good leg, reaching out for the doorjamb to balance himself. "Reasonable ones."

"So we should have reached a truce, but for some

reason we haven't." She tilted her head, ignoring that he was about to fall over. "Why is that?"

Ty gripped the doorjamb more tightly. He was in pain and he wanted her gone so he could deal with it. "*Madeline,* I don't quite know how to say this, so I'm just going to say it. You remind me of things I want to forget."

"Skip?" There was a husky note in her voice that kind of ripped at him.

"I don't want to forget Skip," he said gruffly. "But I think you can figure out the part I do want to forget, and I can't do that while you're here."

"So I should leave so you can forget?" Her eyes narrowed even more. "Maybe you need to work through this issue rather than forgetting. Because like it or not, I'm here. For now."

"And maybe," he said in a deadly tone, "you can keep your need-to's to yourself. I know what I *need* right now and I'm probably not going to get it for another few weeks. Three, to be exact."

He hopped into the house on one foot, feeling stupid, and closed the door as she turned and crossed the porch without a backward glance.

Rescued by Madeline. Did it get any worse than that? He limped into the bedroom, and a few minutes later, as he was pulling the stiff brace up over his knee, heard her car drive by on her way to see Myron about selling the ranch.

Ty focused on the brace. He wasn't in a position to have any say in what she did.

EVERY NERVE IN MADELINE's body was humming from the contact with Ty by the time she got into her car and turned the key in the ignition. It was as if her body was saying, "Yes, please, I'll have some of that," while her brain was saying, "Are you crazy?"

Oh, yes. She had to sever the connection. This would never do. She couldn't have a partner who openly resented her, who could barely say thank-you or meet her eyes—even when she was rescuing him. One she was beginning to find attractive in a purely physical way—who wouldn't?—despite all the reasons not to.

One who resented her because she reminded him of things he'd rather forget.

The ranch was going on the block. She was leaving. No more Ty Hopewell in her life. This situation was getting way too complex.

"Hoo, boy." Myron Crenshaw stared across his desk at Madeline, all his enthusiasm gone. "The Lone Summit ranch. Yes." He tidied up a stack of papers as he spoke, then smoothed a hand over what was left of his thinning hair. In another minute he'd be adjusting his rather colorful tie. Where did someone find a tie hand-painted with a cactus?

"Is that a problem?" Madeline asked pleasantly, while her stomached tightened into a hard little knot. She'd driven almost two hours to get to his office. Now it seemed she'd wasted her time.

"I did handle the previous sale of that property." Myron smiled self-consciously. "I think the property

was listed for more than three years before your...
brother?" Madeline nodded. "Before your brother and
Ty bought the place."

"Was there much interest? I mean, did anyone look
at it during those years? Was the price too high or
what?"

"The location was too isolated. Now, granted, we
may be able to interest someone who doesn't want to
raise cattle, who simply wants a getaway, but the odds
aren't in your favor because there's no power."

"So I've heard."

"It's a beautiful piece of property, but with the lack
of amenities... When the nearest town has a population
of five hundred and the next nearest town a population
of ten thousand, and there's an hour drive between the
two, and then another hour to—"

"I understand the shortcomings. Do you think you
can sell the place?"

"I'll certainly try," he said with a burst of obviously
false enthusiasm. "I do ask for an exclusive, though,
when dealing with properties such as yours."

"Three months?"

He laughed. "Remember, it took me three years last
time."

"You want an indefinite exclusive for a property you
don't think you can sell?"

"I didn't say that." He sounded indignant. "I said it
would take time. I don't want to invest time and energy
only to have the account pulled."

Madeline gathered her purse and stood. "I'll consider your proposition and get back to you."

"I, uh, think you'll find that I'm your best bet." Myron also stood.

"Thank you." And goodbye.

"I'm open until five," Myron called helpfully as Madeline made for the door. She let herself out and stood for a moment on the freshly scraped and sanded sidewalk. Then she crossed the street to the café on the other side.

Three years.

She didn't want to be Ty's partner for three years. Not when she seemed unable to forget the way he'd felt as she'd hauled him to his house.

The man was solid muscle and a lot heavier than she'd expected. He seemed so lean that she'd assumed it'd be easy to get him across the icy yard, but it had taken all she had to keep her feet under her. It hadn't helped that she'd been distracted by his warmth and a rather interesting mix of scents—hay, guy and...rosemary? Or maybe cedar. She hadn't quite identified the spice, but it had been heady stuff when mixed with guy and hay.

Pheromones could be evil at times.

CHAPTER TEN

THE CAFÉ WAS WARM and the scent of freshly baked
cinnamon rolls hit Madeline as soon as she walked
inside. Silk poinsettia centerpieces decorated each
table and small wreaths hung from the sides of the red
vinyl booths. A Christmas tree in the corner had paper
tags on it instead of ornaments. Heaps of presents lay
beneath.

"Hi." The waitress was at the booth almost before
Madeline was seated.

"Hi," she echoed. "I'll have a cinnamon roll and a
cup of coffee.

"I like a woman who knows what she wants," the
woman said as she jotted down the order and tucked
the book back into her apron. "I'll be back in a sec."

Madeline looked around the restaurant. She was the
only person in the place, but it was ten-thirty. Too late
for breakfast and too early for lunch. She left her purse
at the table and walked over to the Christmas tree. The
tags, as she'd expected, had the names and ages of children who needed gifts.

*What do you think, Skip? Boy or girl? Teen or tod-
dler?*

Last year she'd made a donation to the local teen

crisis center in his name. This year she'd been too distracted.

She pulled a tag for a sixteen-year-old boy and another for a thirteen-year-old girl. Most people probably went for the younger kids. Easier to shop for. Madeline liked a challenge.

"Good for you," the waitress said when she returned with the cinnamon roll and coffeepot. "We're hoping to empty that tree by the end of the week, but with hard economic times…" She shook her head and poured the coffee.

"How is the economy here?"

"Well, we're lucky to be in a gold-mining area, so there are still jobs. Ranching is suffering and gaming is way down." The waitress's mouth tightened in a way that made Madeline think that tips were probably down, too. "People are being careful with their money."

"No doubt." Madeline peeled the top off a small container of cream. "Is there a good real-estate agent in town? Or would I be better off going to Elko?"

"There's Myron Crenshaw, right across the street." Madeline smiled politely. "What kind of property are you looking to buy?"

Madeline saw no need to correct her. "A smaller ranch property. Say…a couple hundred acres."

"Myron," the waitress said firmly. "Or you might try Kira Ross. She works from her home, which is about fifty miles from here."

"Fifty miles."

"Yeah." The waitress didn't seem to think that was a

big deal. "She should be in the phone book. I know for a fact she's on the internet because my uncle just bought a lot on the marshes from her."

"Anyone else?"

"Well, you might try Century 21, but the local office mainly does horse properties, not ranches."

"What's a horse property?" Madeline asked, pouring the cream into her coffee. Wasn't a ranch a horse property?

"A piece of land with enough room for a few horses," the waitress explained patiently. "A couple acres."

"I see." Madeline smiled before she picked up the spoon next to her cup. "Thanks for the information."

"Anytime." The waitress sauntered away, stopping to adjust the holiday bouquet on a nearby table before returning to the counter.

Kira Ross was in the phone book and, better than that, she was in town and more than happy to meet with Madeline. Madeline suggested the café and Kira countered with the public library.

"More private," she said with a laugh. "At least until school gets out and it becomes the local babysitting service."

Madeline killed the two hours until the appointment shopping for Christmas presents for the Angel Tree. She bought a couple small gifts—a necklace for the girl, a skater hat with a popular logo for the boy—then added two healthy gift certificates so that the kids could do their own shopping at the local variety store. The clerk wrapped the presents as she chatted with Madeline, who then dropped them off at the café on her way to the library. Her throat closed as she placed the presents under the tree. She wished she'd been shopping with her brother instead of in memory of him.

How would he feel about her selling the ranch?

Would he approve, because she was doing what was best for her? Disapprove, because she wasn't doing what was best for his business partner...who made her nerves tingle and smelled of some as yet unidentified, intriguing spice?

I have to sell, Skip.

The one thing they'd never seen eye to eye on was his quitting his job and, for all intents and purposes, dropping out of society. At least society as Madeline knew it. She'd always figured it was a phase, a sort of late-twenties craziness he needed to get out of his system.

When Madeline entered the children's section of the library, an attractive woman with straight blond hair to her shoulders waved at her before leaning down to say something to two small boys. They nodded solemnly in unison and threw themselves into the beanbag chairs near the window, each with a book.

"Hi," the woman said, holding out a hand and closing the small distance between them. "I'm Kira Ross."

"Madeline Blaine."

Kira led the way to an adult-size table near the wall, private, but still within sight of the children's area. "You want to sell the Lone Summit Ranch?" she asked as soon as they were seated.

"Are you familiar with it?"

"I am. I remember the last time it was on the market. I don't think it'll be an easy sell. It's one of those places that's great for what it's being used for now, but finding people who need it for the same purposes, well, that may take a while."

Exactly what Ty had told her. And Myron, too.

"That doesn't mean it won't sell," Kira continued, "only that it's not a quick and sure deal."

"I understand."

"Are you in a position where you can wait for a sale? Or, if you don't mind me asking, is it a necessity?"

"It's more of a case of wanting to get out." Kira raised her eyebrows and Madeline explained, "I inherited half the property from my brother. I live in New York, and I'm not well versed on ranching, so I think the best move is to sell."

"Your partner?"

"Has agreed to the sale." *He doesn't have much choice.*

Kira blew out a breath, then shot a quick glance over to her boys, who were now snuggled together in one chair, the older one pretending to read to the younger. She focused on Madeline again.

"Forgive me for saying that you don't look like a ranch owner, but for the time being, you're probably going to be one."

Madeline nodded resignedly.

"I'd be happy to come up and look at the property, but

unfortunately, not until January. I'm going to Boise for the holidays. My sister is pregnant and due any day."

Madeline really wished they could have settled matters sooner, but it was hard to compete with a pregnant sister. "I understand. I'll have to arrange to fly back for the meeting." The long drive from Reno again. She shuddered.

"You're not living here now?"

"Visiting."

"I know I'm supposed to be a salesperson and all, but have you considered hanging on to the property? My husband thinks your partner is running a decent operation. What with organic beef coming into vogue, you might be sitting on a gold mine."

"Is your husband a friend of Ty's?" Madeline thought she did an excellent job of keeping suspicion out of her voice, just in case Kira's husband was a friend.

Kira laughed. "No. But the ranching community is tight, so we know one another's business and reputation, even if we aren't close friends."

"What is Ty's reputation?"

Kira blinked at the point-blank question. "My husband was surprised the ranch was going on the block, so I'd say his reputation is good." She tilted her head. "Are you asking me if you can trust him?"

So Kira Ross was a straight talker, too.

"I don't know Ty very well," Madeline explained. "He was my brother's partner. And I don't know anything about ranching, so I haven't been able to assess his... management abilities."

"Then perhaps you should educate yourself," Kira said bluntly. "You'd be in a better position to decide whether or not you really want to sell."

"I've never been in the rural West." Madeline tried to be tactful, just in case Kira's ranch looked like Ty's. "My ranch seems to be…ramshackle."

Kira laughed again. "It doesn't look like the ranch on *Bonanza?*"

Madeline shifted in her seat. Truthfully, she *had* gauged the ranch by what she'd seen on television. "It's not picturesque," she allowed.

"It's probably pretty normal by local standards. Working ranches here tend to be bare-bones. Wood was expensive to haul in, so most of the homesteaders and early ranchers only built what they had to. Nowadays ranchers can put up prefabricated metal buildings and sheds, but if they have an older wood building that will do, why bother? Ask Ty about it."

Oh, yeah. Ty loved it when she asked him questions.

Kira reached into her purse and pulled out a business card. "If you still want to sell, give me a call in January and I'll see what I can do for you."

"I appreciate that."

"So, what do you do in New York?"

"I'm a professor of anthropology."

"*Really.* That sounds fascinating."

Madeline and Kira spent the next several minutes chatting, until the boys wearied of reading and disappeared into the stacks.

"I'd better go help select books," Kira said apologetically.

"Have fun with that." Madeline draped her purse strap over her arm. "I'll call you in January."

If Skip was sending her a message, it was coming in loud and clear through the real-estate agents' dreary sales predictions. But Madeline had every intention of calling Kira. She huffed out a breath as she left the library, as she'd always done when, during an argument, Skip had made a point she didn't agree with.

I can't keep the place. All right?

Madeline was getting into her car for the long drive home when her phone rang. Her heart jumped. Everett? Connor? News?

Her grandmother's name was on the screen.

"Grandma. Is everything all right?" Madeline asked, without bothering to say hello. Her grandmother never made cell-phone calls.

"Why didn't you tell me about your job?"

So much for protecting her grandma. "I didn't want to worry you."

"Because I've had no experience with worry," Eileen replied, with enough of a bite to let Madeline know she was hurt at being left out of the loop.

"It's not that I didn't think you could handle it, it's just that…" Madeline's voice trailed off. She felt as if she was sixteen and had come in after curfew.

"You were ashamed?"

Exactly. "I didn't do anything wrong, but yes. I guess I was ashamed."

"I do not for one minute believe you've done anything wrong."

"Thank you." At least someone besides Connor believed in her. She hadn't exactly received a rally of support from the people she worked with when she'd been suspended—most probably because they didn't want to rub Dr. Mann the wrong way. Madeline had never backed down from an issue, whether it was funding for her student labs, or the ridiculous policy that had tripled the paperwork necessary to submit academic proposals to the department head. She didn't know if her colleagues were distancing themselves so they wouldn't get dragged down with her, or because they believed she was guilty. "I planned to tell you after the investigation. I didn't want to ruin the holidays and cause concern." She paused, then asked, "How'd you find out?"

"It's on the internet."

"But only if you go looking for it." A small college in a midsize university suspending academic staff wasn't exactly earthshaking news that the wires picked up. Jensen's situation had hit the local papers, so Eileen was aware of *his* troubles, but thankfully Madeline's suspension hadn't made print.

"To tell you the truth, Connor's been acting shifty, and when I questioned him, he was quite uncomfortable. I figured it had to have something to do with you."

Madeline rolled her eyes. Connor was a worse liar than she was.

"It took me a while, but I finally got a general idea of where to start my research."

"So he didn't break under your interrogation."

Her grandmother laughed. "No. He sputtered at the proper moments." Her voice became serious again when she said, "I think it was a good idea to visit Skip's property rather than stay here and obsess over matters you can't control. But you should have told me the entire truth."

"Agreed," Madeline said in resignation. She should have told her. But it had been so damned embarrassing....

"Tell me about the ranch Skip was so proud of." Eileen, like Madeline, had never understood what possessed Skip, the favorite grandchild, to throw away his education and take up ranching.

"I'm selling."

"Mr. Hopewell made an offer?"

"Not exactly." Her grandmother made no response, waiting. So Madeline poured out her frustrations about the condition of the ranch and how she and Ty hadn't exactly hit it off, which was an understatement bordering on a lie. The only solution was to sell and go on with her life and leave Ty to his.

When she was done, there was a long silence, and then her grandmother said, "Are you being fair to Mr. Hopewell?"

Madeline almost dropped the phone. "Fair how?" she asked in disbelief. Her grandmother had hammered fairness into her since birth. Later in life, Madeline had learned that even though she might be playing fair, oftentimes the rest of the world wasn't. But that was no excuse to Eileen. One played fair at all times.

"He's shouldered the burden of running the ranch alone, since Skip passed away."

"He gets an extra percentage for that burden, Grandma. And he's agreed to sell. I want to sell. I think that adds up to, well, selling."

"It's a big decision, and not to be made lightly."

"Grandma—"

"You're under pressure because of your job. It makes perfect sense to try to extract yourself from other complications. But this may not be the time to make such a decision."

Okay, this was getting weird. Why on earth was her grandmother, the most sensible of women, taking this track? Madeline was about to ask when Eileen started to speak, then stopped abruptly to clear her throat, not once, but twice.

Her grandmother, who *never* cried, was on the edge of tears.

Oh. Dear. Heavens. Madeline felt like such a fool.

She pressed the heel of her palm against her forehead. Eileen wasn't ready for this step. She wasn't ready to let go of this last link to Skip.

"I'll tell you what," Madeline said finally, in as steady a voice as she could manage. "I'll give the matter more thought. Maybe I should familiarize myself more thoroughly with the situation."

"I thought that was the reason you're there," her grandmother managed to say.

"It is. I just...got sidetracked."

"I simply want you to be sure you have all the data," Eileen said with a note of huskiness in her voice.

"I'll get more data," Madeline agreed, feeling both trapped and guilty. "And I'll be home on Christmas Eve, as planned, and we'll talk then."

She hung up a few minutes later and then let her head drop back against the seat rest.

She hadn't seen this one coming.

CHAPTER ELEVEN

TY HAD JUST FINISHED washing his few dishes when Alvin lifted his head off his paws.

"Do we have a visitor?" he asked the dog. Just what he needed. He was almost to the door when Madeline knocked.

"Come in," he said, stepping back. A subzero cold front was moving in on the heels of the warm front that had dumped snow the day before, and he didn't want to spar with Madeline in an open doorway.

"Thank you." She ducked past him, then stopped inside the door. "How's your knee?" she asked politely.

"Better now that it's in the brace." The tension hummed between them.

"I got back from town a few minutes ago," she said, as if she hadn't driven by his place. Ty waited, knowing she'd speak her piece without encouragement from him. "According to the real-estate agents, we're going to be partners for eternity, because this place will never sell."

He didn't say "I told you so," but it was tempting. "Are you going to put it on the market anyway?"

She glanced down at the floor briefly. "I initially

came to the ranch to understand more about the operation. Instead of doing that, I allowed myself to get off track."

She'd also sidestepped his question. He wanted an answer. "So what does all this boil down to?" Because it was boiling down to something.

Madeline raised her chin. "I'm going to help you with chores tomorrow."

Ty blinked. The hell she was. "I'm not that injured."

"Are you going to be able to drive the tractor with your knee like that?"

Good question—one he'd been asking himself. The last time his knee had gone out, the cows were on pasture and he hadn't had to drive the tractor and deal with the clutch.

"If I can't, I'll hire someone to help." Manny Hernandez, the local handyman, was always up for a job.

"You'd hire someone when you can have me help for free? No wonder the ranch isn't making any money."

"Madeline—"

"I'm sorry," she blurted, cutting him off. "I wasn't trying to go for the jugular. I just…have some stuff on my mind."

"Yeah. I imagine you do." For a moment she said nothing, but he could see the wheels turning.

"You researched me," she finally said in a flat voice.

"I did."

"What did you find out?"

"That you're probably as interested in lying low as you are in selling the ranch."

She forced a laugh. She was as bad at acting as she was at lying. "You think I'm here because I'm running away from an uncomfortable situation?" He raised an eyebrow. "I'm taking advantage of the time off to do something I should have done last summer."

"Why didn't you do it last summer?"

"I had summer classes."

"And now you have no classes."

"Until January."

"That's not what the article said. Indefinite suspension."

Madeline's back seemed to become even straighter than before. The woman had excellent posture. "The hearing is immediately after New Year's. I'll be teaching when the semester starts. My lawyer assures me it's more of a formality than anything."

"Yet they suspended you."

"I don't get along with the department head," she announced candidly, holding Ty's gaze, daring him to make something of it. "I believe she took the opportunity to try to teach me who wields the power."

"Have you learned a lesson?" he asked drily.

"Look," Madeline snapped, "my private affairs are exactly that. I'm here to discuss chores tomorrow."

"Why do you need to understand the operation if you're going to sell?" It seemed like a reasonable question to him, but a look of pure frustration crossed her features. "What?"

"I don't know."

Funny. He thought she knew everything.

She glanced down at the floor for such a long time that he didn't think she was going to answer. Finally she lifted her chin, shaking her hair back over her shoulders. "I'm trying to understand what my brother found so fascinating about this lifestyle. I just don't get it."

Ty felt a wallop to his midsection and hoped it didn't show on his face.

"And my grandmother...she's having issues letting go. I want to know enough about the ranch so I can answer her questions. And maybe my own, as well."

Oh, shit. No way around this one. He pulled in a breath. "Can you drive a tractor?"

Madeline hesitated only a moment. "Sure."

"It'll be cold. Dress warm."

She smirked. "I'm from the Northeast."

"And you're going to be sitting on a metal tractor seat for an hour. Dress warm."

MADELINE WAS READY TO GO when Ty knocked on her door the next morning, and, frankly, nervous about what the morning might bring. She didn't want to screw up.

When she opened the door, Ty handed her a bulky cloth bundle.

"Put that on. You'll be warmer when we feed."

Madeline stared at the heavy brown fabric in her hands. "I'm fine," she said. She didn't want to wear Ty's clothing. It seemed too intimate.

"You'll freeze your ass off."

"It's mine to freeze."

"You can't go out in these temperatures wearing a puffy coat with little sissy gloves." She opened her mouth to protest, but he added, "I don't want to have to interrupt feeding to bring you back when frostbite starts setting in."

He turned and walked toward the barn without another word, the dog following at his heels. Madeline closed the door and shook out the coveralls, assessing. Big. Way too big. But she'd make them work. She could still feel the bite of the frigid air from the few minutes the door had stood open, and knew it'd be stupid not to wear the coveralls, which were clean if oil-stained.

When she put them on, the sleeves hung off the ends of her hands, but she was able to push them up far enough to let her fingers see the light of day before she shoved them into the large leather gloves he'd had wrapped inside the rolled coveralls. She zipped the garment to her chin, then stepped into her fleece-lined leather boots.

One quick look in the mirror on the wall behind the built-in bookcase confirmed her suspicions. She did indeed look like the Michelin man's long-lost twin sister.

Screw it.

Madeline set her shoulders and headed for the door.

TY LOOKED UP and then quickly back down when Madeline entered the barn, where the tractor was idling. He tried not to laugh. Truly he did, because he was in a grim mood and had no intention of interacting with her any more than necessary.

"Oh, shut up," Madeline snapped as she walked toward the tractor. "This wasn't my idea."

He held his hands up in a gesture of surrender, but it had been so long since he'd found humor in anything, he couldn't wipe the grin off his face as he stood back to let her climb into the driver's seat.

"What goes around comes around," she muttered before taking a moment to familiarize herself with the pedals and levers. She looked up at him. "What do I do first?"

His smile disappeared. "I thought you said you could drive a tractor."

"I can. I just don't know how to get it moving."

"You need a driving lesson?" he asked, incredulous.

"I need instruction in what the levers and pedals do. Driving is simply a matter of turning the wheel," Madeline said in an academic tone. "And *I* don't have a bum knee, so *I* can push in the clutch, unlike someone else I know."

Ty felt the beginning of a headache. He could push in a clutch if he had to. But it was just going to be a slow, painful process. Not real good for the clutch mechanism, either.

He silently acknowledged he'd been had. But what the hell? If she wanted to learn to drive the tractor, she owned half of it. Why not? It would be nigh impossible for even the worst driver to screw up driving a straight line across a field in low gear.

"That's the throttle," he said patiently, pointing to the lever on the column. "You have two pedals to control the wheels…" He explained the operation of the machine, the gauges, etc. Not that she needed to know, but because she insisted on knowing. Then he asked her if she was ready to give it a shot.

She nodded and put the engine in gear. Ty stayed standing on the running board in case of emergency, but Madeline, after a jerky start, adeptly maneuvered the tractor out of the barn and with very little direction pulled up next to the haystack, exactly where he needed it to be.

"Not bad, eh?" she asked.

"You're a natural," Ty agreed, feeling an odd sensation when she glanced up at him.

"You don't need to be sarcastic," she muttered.

"I wasn't."

She sent him a sidelong glance. "Really?"

"Yeah." He wasn't exactly comfortable with this side of Madeline. He wasn't comfortable with any side of Madeline but this side was more disturbing than the annoying know-it-all.

She insisted on helping him load the trailer, and he let her drag bales way too heavy for her because it was easier than trying to stop her. He showed her how to stab the hay hooks into the dried alfalfa, then together they could maneuver the bales into the growing stack on the trailer. He had to admit that having her help was saving his knee.

Once the hay was loaded, he pointed her out into the field, explaining how she was to drive slowly while he cut the bale strings and tossed hay off the side.

The cows were waiting, and mobbed the trailer as she drove through the second gate Ty opened. Alvin snapped and barked, performing his routine with full border-collie enthusiasm. Madeline glanced at him over her shoulder, frowning at the dog's ferocity. She waited for Ty to climb awkwardly back on the trailer before directing her attention forward again.

Ty had forgotten what it was like not to have to fight the cattle off as he tossed bales. The feeding, which usually took an hour, was done in forty-five minutes. Madeline came to a stop a good twenty yards from the last bale. Ty eased himself off the trailer and walked up to the tractor, where he climbed onto the running board. Alvin stood wide-legged and victorious on his trailer.

"Head back to the barn," Ty instructed, leaning close so she could hear him over the noise of the motor. "Follow those tracks so we don't get stuck." He pointed to the trail of beaten-down snow he always followed. Madeline nodded and gave the throttle a turn. The tractor lurched forward and Ty automatically grabbed the back of her seat as she shifted gears. Madeline shot him a sidelong glance, a spark of exhilaration in her eyes as the engine roared louder and the machine picked up speed. He stared straight ahead, hoping she wouldn't drive off the track into the fence or anything.

Ty's fingers were cramped from hanging on by the time Madeline pulled into the barn. She turned off the engine with a show of satisfaction. He pried his fingers loose.

"Uh, thanks for the help," he said, easing himself to the ground. Alvin jumped off the trailer and stood waiting for phase two of the chores.

"We're not done yet, are we?"

"We're done with the tractor, and that's what you hired on for."

"But—"

"Thanks for the help, Maddie."

She gave him a look, making it clear that for once she wasn't going to waste her time arguing with him, but that she thought he was a fool.

Maybe he was, but when he was with her, his thoughts about the ranch, the wreck…her…jumbled together. He'd decided yesterday, after she'd rescued him, that the anger that evoked was the worst because it, in turn, fueled more guilt. What right did he have to be angry?

He watched her walk away in those ridiculous coveralls.

What right did he have to find her attractive?

MADELINE HAD FULLY EXPECTED feeding to be a chore she'd have to endure. Cold weather, large unfamiliar animals, a taciturn man who didn't like having her around. Instead she'd gotten a kick out of driving the tractor. The novelty would undoubtedly wear off within the next few days, but right now she felt satisfied. And cold. Very cold.

She was chilled through by the time she climbed the porch steps to her house. The generator came to life and the lights came on. Madeline turned on the furnace and stood over a vent for a couple minutes before unzipping the coveralls and heading for the bathroom. She cranked on the faucet, then after a few seconds, set the plug and left the bath to fill.

She was pulling her arms out of the coveralls when the generator sputtered a couple times and died.

The overhead light went out, warm air ceased to blow out of the furnace vents, and Madeline automatically reached out and turned off the water.

She sat on the edge of the tub and regarded her folded hands. People had lived for centuries without electricity. She was tough. And disciplined. Yes, she was.

The generator came back on without warning. No cough. No chug. The lights came on. The heat started to blow.

Madeline's shoulders sank in relief, but seconds later the power went off again.

She raised her eyes to the ceiling. "Gee," she said aloud. "I wonder why I want to sell?"

She was sitting, morose and chilled, on the edge of the tub, waiting for a miracle, when Ty knocked on the door. Since the generator was ominously silent, she had a feeling this was not her miracle.

"No power?" she asked, after motioning Ty in and quickly closing the door.

"No fuel. The tank was lower than I thought and the delivery guy didn't show up yesterday like he was supposed to."

"So what now?" she asked, trying to put on a brave face.

"I'm going to siphon some out of my tank into yours."

"Do you need help?"

An odd expression crossed his face before he shook his head.

"How long will it take?"

"Maybe an hour?"

"Can I use your shower?" Surely his house had two bathrooms like hers did. "You won't even know I've been there." But she wanted to be there. She had itchy particles of hay in her clothing and she was chilled. She wanted a shower.

"Sure."

She wondered if there was any way he could have made the word sound any less sincere. "I appreciate it." She grabbed her towel and toiletries and stuffed them into her bathroom tote.

"It'll take me a while to do this, so you don't have to hurry."

"But I will," she said.

TY WORKED SLOWLY, making sure it took him at least an hour to siphon fuel into containers, carry them to her tank, climb the ladder, which was a slow process anyway because of the knee brace, and pour them in.

Plenty of time for her to shower. He didn't mind, he just didn't want to be there when she did it. Having her in his house, showering, was too…intimate.

Would he feel that way if Becky Morris, the vet's new assistant, needed to shower off after a nasty tussle with a cow?

Probably not. But he didn't notice stuff about her that he noticed about Madeline.

As SHE'D PROMISED, Madeline hurried through her shower, but there was no way she could hurry through drying and ironing her hair, so she pulled it back while it was still wet and secured it in a barrette. Already tendrils were curling around her face.

Her hair drove her insane. She had hated her curls forever, but it was more than that. People didn't seem to take her seriously when she was both short and curly-headed. Straighten those curls out into silky, well-disciplined strands and voilà, instant respect. Okay, maybe not *instant* respect, but her hair no longer distracted people. They no longer hid smiles on bad-hair days, which were almost every day when she didn't use the flatiron.

Madeline pulled the barrette out and plugged in her hair dryer. She wanted out of here before Ty came back, but she knew from long experience her hair tamed better damp. She twisted a strand around her finger in weary disgust, then grabbed her brush and started the daily routine.

Madeline left the bathroom twenty minutes later.

She'd kept the door cracked open, so she could hear if Ty came in, but the house was still empty when she walked down the hall to the austere living room. Transferring fuel took longer than she had expected and a quick glance out the window explained why. Ty was climbing down a ladder leaned against her fuel tank, carrying a yellow fuel container in one hand.

Oh, that had to be a lot of fun with his damaged knee, brace or no brace. How many trips had he made?

She slipped into her coat and wrapped the scarf around her neck. One of her gloves fell off the counter, and when she stooped down to pick it up, she noticed a collection of colored envelopes in the trash.

Green envelopes, red ones, cream-colored with gold edging.

Christmas cards.

The top one wasn't even opened. Madeline nudged it with her index finger, feeling guilty for prying, but maybe he'd used a letter opener and… No, it wasn't slit open. It was sealed, as were the five envelopes below it.

Madeline stood, a frown on her face. This bothered her.

Who threw away Christmas cards? Unopened Christmas cards?

She jumped a mile when the door opened behind her, and she whirled around. She obviously looked guilty, since Ty asked, "What?"

"Are those Christmas cards?" she asked, pointing at the trash.

He didn't answer. He didn't have to.

"I don't understand...."

"You don't need to understand."

Madeline made a small gesture of frustration. "Ty, if those people took the time—"

"Those people mean well. I appreciate that they took the time to think of me."

"But you throw the cards away unopened."

"They'll never know."

Madeline was stunned. "That is so cold." As was his expression.

"I don't do Christmas, all right? They know that."

"You don't do Christmas," she echoed. "Why?"

"Why the hell do you think?" he asked impatiently.

It took her a second to get it. "The accident?"

"Yeah. The accident." He didn't mock her, didn't speak with one hint of irony in his voice, yet somehow Madeline felt stupid.

"So you boycott Christmas. That makes a lot of sense."

"You deal with loss your way, I'll deal with it in mine."

That wasn't dealing with loss. It was denial. "Ty—"

"Enough, Madeline." His expression was so deadly serious that the words she'd been about to say died on her lips.

As he'd said. Enough. "I'm sorry. I dropped a glove and...I honestly wasn't going through your trash."

Ty looked past her at the trash can, where the envelopes sat in plain view. Then he nodded.

"I'll, uh, see you later. Thanks for the shower. And the fuel."

"Anytime," he replied, his voice distant.

Ty was trying to hide it, but it was easy to read the discomfort in his expression and the fact that he wanted her gone. Now. She didn't say another word as she left the house and stepped out into the ultrabrisk air.

She barely felt it.

Ty didn't celebrate *Christmas,* because of the accident.

She'd assumed that he had worked through the painful issues over the past twenty-odd months. As she had. After all, she'd lost a brother, and she'd deal with what had happened. For the most part.

Ty obviously hadn't. No wonder he had barriers up where she was concerned. She was a living reminder of an incident he had yet to deal with, and the second anniversary of it was rapidly approaching.

Two years had passed and Ty Hopewell was still hurting.

CHAPTER TWELVE

TY WENT TO TOWN that afternoon. He simply got in his truck and left, for the first time since Madeline had arrived. She hoped he got his mail.

A pickup truck loaded with wood showed up shortly after he left. The man tossed the wood onto a tarp he'd spread next to the trailer, chucking one piece after another, and then he left, without payment, before she realized he was gone.

Madeline opened the trailer door as the truck drove to the gate, surveying the mound of precious wood. She needed to get a fire going as quickly as possible.

There was an ax in the barn, hanging on the equipment wall. She slipped into her boots and retrieved it, and then awkwardly cut some kindling, glad Ty was off the property for this show. Ax work had never been her forte, and after a trip to the emergency room when she was fourteen to stitch up a sliced shin, her grandmother had strongly suggested that Skip handle the ax from that point on. Madeline had happily agreed, but now wished she'd had more practice. Her kindling was roughly the size of her wrist. She split those pieces again without mishap, breathing a sigh of relief as she returned the tool to the barn with all her fingers intact. She should have cut more, but for now, she was happy not to be traveling to the emergency room.

She dumped the kindling on the floor next to the stove, crumpled up some printer paper and built a fire. Skip may have handled the ax, but Madeline had taken care of the fire in her grandmother's beast of a stove.

Printer paper didn't burn well, but after peeling off shreds of wood and coaxing them to a flame along with the paper, she was able to add kindling. It was only after she had the fire going that she thought about bird nests in the stovepipe. But the fire took hold and smoke exited the chimney, exactly as it should.

Satisfied, she went back outside and started piling the wood into neat stacks—a small one on the porch next to the door for easy access and the rest on the tarp next to the trailer. She'd have to purchase another tarp to cover the pile, unless Ty had one, but for the moment the skies were clear.

Madeline carried two more pieces of wood into the house and stoked the fire, then immediately went to work on the book. She made a decent amount of headway as the fire quickly warmed the house. Probably because her fingers weren't half-frozen. Amazing what heat did for the mental processes.

Every now and then, though, her fingers would grow still and she'd think about Ty. And the Christmas cards. Since she knew his pain, it made her heart ache.

SHE'D STACKED THE WOOD.

Ty had planned on piling it himself once he got back

from the trip to town he'd put off for too long. For once it felt good to get off the ranch, mingle anonymously with people in the stores in Wesley, even if he could have done without the holiday joy.

Well, more power to her. The house now had a twenty-four-hour heat source, and the fuel company promised delivery no later than tomorrow, so she could run the old generator twelve hours a day if she wanted to risk a breakdown. And then Madeline was on her own for however long she planned to be here.

He wished she was on her own somewhere else.

He'd been perpetually on edge since she'd showed up at the ranch, but now that they'd opened the subject of the wreck and she'd discovered one of his ways of dealing with it, he felt even edgier. As if his survival strategies would disintegrate under close scrutiny.

It took almost twenty minutes to unload the truck. That was his penance for rarely leaving the ranch. He'd spent quite a bit of time at the hardware and feed store, not so much at the grocery store, which had been his last stop. When he'd gotten there he'd been tired and anxious to get home, so he'd bought only the bare essentials, planning to stock up at a later date at Anne McKirk's mercantile. Now, as he opened a microwave dinner, he kind of wished he'd bought more.

After eating, he grabbed an oil filter and a gallon jug of 15W-40 to service his generator. He had time before the light faded, and it would keep his mind busy.

The generator house was just large enough to hold the machine and the guy working on it, with a little room for Alvin if he curled up in the corner. Alvin chose to stay outside on the path and watch for coyotes, who were sneaking in closer now that food was scarce in the snow.

Ty removed the faceplate from the machine, then sat on the frigid concrete slab and started to work with his socket wrench. Two seconds later a shadow fell across the machine. He didn't even bother to look over his shoulder. Unless Alvin had grown several inches, or one of the cows had gotten out, it had to be Madeline.

She stood silently behind him as he worked, and he felt ultra-aware of her. Was she here to hash things out? If so, what things? Christmas cards, or ranching, or what?

His fingers were stiff and clumsy from the cold, and having her watch every move he made wasn't helping his dexterity. He dropped a nut, found it next to his leg, then tried to thread it back onto the bolt again.

"How often do you have to service these machines?"

He was relieved that she finally spoke. "Every three hundred hours of operation."

"Frequently, then."

"About once a month." He looked over his shoulder. She was standing in the doorway, hands in her pockets and a stocking cap on her head. For once he had no idea what she was thinking or why she was there. He reached for the wrench and went back to work.

"Thank you for the wood."

"No problem." He tightened a bolt.

"How much do I owe you?"

"I'll take it out of the ranch funds."

"Mind if I watch?"

"Knock yourself out," he said without looking at her. The concrete was getting cold under his ass and he still had to drain the oil. "Are you here for any other reason?"

"Some questions about the ranch, but I can wait until you're done."

Fine. As long as they stuck to talking about the ranch, he'd play ball. The minute she eased into personal territory—conversation over.

MADELINE WATCHED TY work on the machine, his bare hands turning red from the cold. When he finished he pulled his gloves back on and picked up the container of used oil and the old oil filter.

"Do you recycle?"

He led her around to the back of the generator building and showed her how he poured the used oil into a drum. "I take the drums to the plant in Reno once a year. I collect a couple barrels with all the machinery."

She liked knowing that he ran a clean operation.

They walked to the barn together. Ty opened the door, gesturing for her to go in ahead of him. Alvin waited behind him, apparently afraid of being locked in an enclosed space with her again. Once Ty came through, the dog followed.

"I'm curious," she said, watching him cut open a

hay bale, then fill a manger. "You're following Skip's business plan, but the economy has changed. So..."

Now that she was looking for it, she could sense the change in him when she mentioned her brother's name. She leaned a shoulder against the straw stack, which she'd already learned wasn't as bristly as the haystack.

"I've adjusted accordingly. Skip's plan had more immediate expansion, but I've cut back for now. In fact, I've brought us close to the point Skip and I started at."

"You've been putting enough money back into the place that you're barely breaking even," she pointed out.

"In this economy that's not bad. A lot of bigger operations are losing money." For once he didn't seem to take offense at her questioning his business practices. Perhaps it was the way she was doing it... "If I *don't* put money into the place, it's going to get away from me, but for the past four months, I haven't reinvested anything." A corner of his mouth quirked up. "I didn't want to lose money, you see."

Ty took a pitchfork out of a bale and started forking the soiled bedding into a wheelbarrow. "I," he said, stabbing the fork into the straw with more force than was probably necessary, "have done everything possible to break even. I've culled stock to reduce feeding costs. I've stopped overall ranch improvements temporarily, which is why the roof on the equipment shed isn't finished." *Ah, the hole in the corner where the snow was accumu-*

lating. He flung a forkful of straw into the barrow, and then another. "I haven't taken any kind of a salary."

"You've taken *no* salary."

He stopped tossing straw for a moment and leaned on the pitchfork. "I've bought food, paid the utilities and fuel bills. Other than that, no. Nothing in savings, or retirement. I haven't bought so much as a pair of Wranglers in the past year."

Well, that explained the rather fascinating wear patterns she'd noticed.

"Any more questions?" Ty asked stiffly. Had he followed the direction of her thoughts? She rather hoped not.

The cow stamped a hoof as she dealt with a frustrating clump of hay. They turned in unison to look at her and she stamped again. A front foot. The back end of her didn't budge.

"If she doesn't get better soon, then…?" Madeline made a slicing gesture across her throat.

"'Fraid so." Ty's dark eyes met hers and she thought she saw regret.

"Sad."

"This is a ranch, Madeline." From the way he spoke, she wondered if he'd heard those words himself a long time ago.

Ty stuck the fork back into the bale, then filled the cow's water container as Madeline considered the harsh reality of ranch life. Yes, she ate meat. Yes, she knew where that meat came from. She just wasn't used to staring her dinner in the eye.

When Ty had finished tending to the cow, she said, "Would you mind giving me a schedule of operations for the ranch and a copy of all the financial stuff I didn't see during our meeting? For my grandmother?"

"You mean the meeting where you told me you were going to sell the ranch?"

"Yes," Madeline replied evenly, her gaze shifting down to his mouth. "That meeting." She forced her eyes upward.

Nothing had changed between them, other than her new insight into the hell he seemed to be going through. But because of that, she was going to make an effort to be patient. Put their relationship on friendlier ground, so that when they did have to make mutual business decisions, it wasn't a battlefield.

She might even see what she could do to make herself an ally rather than an enemy. Ty looked as if he could use an ally.

"Come by the house in about an hour," Ty said. "After I've had time to wash the oil off and change. We'll go over the stuff then."

"I'll be there."

MADELINE SHOWED UP exactly an hour later with what was left of Anne's wine. Ty let her into his house and she set the bottle at the center of the table.

"You're kidding," he said, eyeing the bottle, which was well more than half-full. He would have thought she'd learned her lesson.

"Between the two of us we should be fine." When

Ty frowned, she added, "I didn't think it would hurt to relax as we talk."

Relaxing was not what he had in mind. Ty regarded her for a moment, still frowning, then went to the cupboard and pulled down two small jelly jars.

"I'm a bachelor," he said when her eyebrows went up as he set one in front of where she stood next to the table.

"Even bachelors have glassware," she replied, taking a seat.

"Not this one." He uncorked the wine and poured each of them half a jar, with the objective of keeping his wits about him. Anne's wine had an alcohol content that was beyond the legal limit. "Maybe before we start, I'd like to set a few ground rules."

"What kind of ground rules?"

"We stick to ranch business."

"As opposed to…?" Madeline asked innocently.

He narrowed his eyes, but instead of replying, pulled a sheaf of papers off the counter.

"Let's take a look at what happened over the past two years." Madeline nodded, shifting her chair closer as Ty started explaining the figures on the sheets. When he was done and she assured him she understood enough to withstand a grilling from her grandmother, she asked about the yearly schedule of operations. Again he reached over to the counter, only this time retrieved a calendar with the red-and-white-checkered Purina design on the bottom.

"Everything you need to know is here. You can even make a copy for your grandmother."

MADELINE COULDN'T help it. She laughed. The thought of handing Eileen a copy of a Purina calendar and telling her it was the basis of the ranch operations...well, perhaps then her grandmother would see the wisdom of putting the place on the market.

"And this is funny why?" Ty asked, leaning back in his chair and reaching for his jelly glass.

Madeline refrained from asking why he didn't use a computer for scheduling, and instead flipped through the months, reading the notations in various squares. Vaccinations, bulls released, branding, preg checks. A.I.

"A.I.?" she asked, raising her eyes.

"Artificial insemination. I'm adjusting the breeding program and didn't want to buy another bull. Semen is cheaper."

"I see." Where did he get the semen and how...? She shook off the thought and continued to read, taking her time. Some months were packed with notations, while others, the winter months, had markedly fewer.

"I note all the sales on there, but they're also in the records I send to your accountant."

Madeline nodded as she read. "Do you lose many calves?"

"No, thankfully. When you feed a cow all year and then get nothing for your money, it's bad. Financially, that is. A lot of expenditure and no return on your money."

Madeline glanced up, and for once Ty expanded on his answer without being prodded. "If I have a cow that doesn't produce two years in a row, or that has calving difficulties, I send her down the road."

"Down the road?"

Ty slid a finger across his throat.

"Oh."

"We can't afford charity in this business."

"The cow in the sling?"

"Is a good producer. I'm hoping this is a onetime thing. Sam says it's possible, so I'll give her another year."

So the rancher had a heart. Madeline asked a few more questions about the calendar, then, since there was a printer-scanner sitting on the desk in the living room, she asked if he could make her a copy. It would help her explain matters to her grandmother. Not what Skip had found so fascinating, but how the ranch worked.

She settled back in her chair, raised her glass to her lips. It was almost empty, and when she put it back down, Ty automatically poured. She really did like his hands. They were wide and strong. Capable looking. What were they capable of?

"I'll study the calendar more closely when I get home tonight. I want to know what all the equipment is and what it does. How much each costs a year to keep and maintain."

"All right."

"Could you can show me around after we feed tomorrow?"

"I don't know if I'll need help tomorrow." He sounded certain that he wouldn't.

Madeline took another drink. "I think you will," she assured him.

"Maybe you're wrong."

"Maybe I'm tired of spending all my time snowbound in my house."

He smiled. "Maybe you should go back to New York." His eyes held hers in a way that made her very aware of it being just the two of them, here, alone.

"Maybe my lawyer would kill me," Madeline said, glancing at the bottle, which produced such interesting effects on both of their inhibitions. The hand-lettered label on the bottle read Amuma.

"Basque for grandmother," Ty said, answering her un-asked question. Madeline couldn't think of anyone less grandmotherly than Anne McKirk, who she suspected made this wine. "Why would your lawyer kill you?"

"Because—" she pressed her lips together momentarily before admitting the hard truth "—I've been driving him crazy."

"No!" Ty replied, deadpan.

"It's true. When I have an idea I call him." She rather appreciated the glimmer of humor she saw in Ty's expression. It was gone too soon. "I have good ideas."

"Like this wine, for instance."

"Like this wine," she agreed. One glass had given her a faint and pleasant buzz, but nothing like her last buzz after two much larger glasses. "This is the most relaxed conversation we've ever had."

"You're right." He idly moved his glass in a small circle on the table, watching the wine swirl before he looked up at her. "Tell me about your job. What happened?"

Normally Madeline would have instantly tensed at the mention of her job, but right now, thanks to Amuma, she didn't. Yes, this wine was good stuff. "I'm collateral damage."

"Not involved at all."

"Only by association. I worked with Dr. Jensen up until a year ago. He's the one being sued, along with the college, for using blood samples he wasn't authorized to use."

"I read the articles. Can't really blame the people for suing."

"I don't. I just don't like being accused for no other reason than association."

"It seems kind of harsh to me, suspending you just because you worked with someone, even if your department head has it in for you."

"I don't know that for a fact," Madeline admitted. "But I have worked very closely with Dr. Jensen. He was my major professor and my mentor. He helped me get my job at the college."

"Has he tried to exonerate you?"

She wished. "He can't do that."

"Why not?"

"Because there are other circumstances."

Ty regarded her for a long moment. "Such as?"

"I don't know," Madeline admitted. "Legal circumstances. His lawyer won't let him talk to me or about me before the hearing, so..." She shrugged. "There you go."

"Guilty until proven innocent."

"It seems that way." Madeline pulled the calendar toward her again. "So you're following Skip's business plan and the calendar explains everything."

"Will that satisfy your grandmother?"

Madeline met his eyes squarely. "It'll help. I think all she really needs is a little more time to get used to the idea of severing this last link to Skip. She has to come to understand that the ranch isn't Skip."

Ty was working to show no reaction to what she'd just said, but the very fact that he refused to show emotion when Skip's name was mentioned was telling.

"Ty," she said gently. "It was an accident."

He contemplated the glass in his hand, then his mouth tightened as he pulled in a deep, audible breath. He exhaled without saying a word. A second later he emptied the last of his wine, setting the glass on the table with a thump. His expression was once again coolly impassive.

Apparently Amuma had limited powers.

TY CLOSED THE DOOR behind Madeline and went back into the kitchen, which felt oddly empty now that she was gone. He picked up the bottle of Amuma, considered drinking the last few swallows, then upended the bottle and drained it down the sink. He didn't need more wine. He needed…hell, he didn't know what.

Things were certainly easier when he was alone and people like Madeline weren't poking at wounds that needed to be left untouched.

Did he deserve to have things easy? To heal? Could he heal? Maybe not.

Having Madeline here made his situation more difficult. Complex. He was drawn to her, pure and simple. And that wasn't going to work the way he was now.

He really, really wished he'd done as Skip had asked two years ago.

CHAPTER THIRTEEN

TY WOKE UP THE NEXT MORNING feeling a deep need to be alone. His knee was nowhere near one hundred percent, but he'd taped it under the brace and he could run the tractor if he had to. And if he was quiet about it, he might get out into the field before Madeline showed up.

He'd just started the beast, with Alvin in position on the trailer, when the door near the generator opened and Madeline came in, wearing the coveralls.

"I can handle the tractor," Ty said, more dismissively than he'd intended. Yesterday had had enough unsettling contact for a while.

"Then I'll throw the hay."

"You're not getting it, Madeline. My knee is better. I can feed alone."

"No doubt." She leveled a look at him that she probably used to melt uncooperative students.

What the hell. He'd come to the conclusion last night that he didn't deserve things to be easier.

Ty got out of the driver's seat and climbed back off the tractor, grimacing slightly when he banged his knee on the oversize fender.

Madeline flinched emphatically, but said nothing as

she took his place in the seat. Ty headed out the door to the big haystack under the roof, walking as normally as possible with the stiff brace on his leg. Madeline followed with the tractor. Alvin barked away, apparently unconcerned as to who was driving, as long as the trailer moved.

Again Madeline helped load hay, and again Ty knew that his knee was better off because of her help. She said nothing, apparently finally understanding that he wasn't going to talk. Either that or she was biding her time. When she pointed the tractor toward the gate Ty felt himself relax an iota.

Okay, so far, so good. He could do this.

Once they were done and Madeline maneuvered the tractor back onto the road leading between pastures, Ty assumed his spot on the running board, almost as if to prove to himself that he could be close to her and not react. She glanced over at him and said, "Do you mind if I open her up?"

"Uh…" Ty grabbed the back of the seat as Madeline cranked the throttle. She laughed as the tractor picked up speed, and Ty watched her in profile with more fascination that he wanted to feel. This was the second time she'd done this.

"How fast does it go?"

"You're about topped out," he yelled over the wind. Topped out for the gear she was in, that is, but he wasn't going to tell her that. Didn't want her putting them into Overdrive.

Madeline shot a sideways look at him, smiling

with the sheer joy of the moment, and his heart gave a slight bump.

Shit. This was bad.

"Slow down, Madeline."

"Am I scaring you?"

"Yes," he said honestly. But not in the way she thought.

"Oh." She let up on the throttle and the tractor slowed to a feeding-speed crawl. The accident. She thought he was thinking about the accident.

He leaned closer so he didn't have to yell, which was a mistake because she smelled very, very good. Lemon mixed with flowers. "I'm not really scared, but I do have a pen of hungry bulls and horses to feed."

"Fine." She gave the tractor a bit more gas, but the reckless abandonment was gone. Good. He wasn't quite sure how to deal with it.

Give a woman a tractor and she goes wild. Go figure.

IT WAS RELATIVELY WARM, in the high thirties, so Madeline pulled off her stocking cap and shook out her hair. The cap smelled of exhaust, so she stuffed it into her oversize pocket. She'd wash it in the sink before feeding again.

"I meant to tell you yesterday that you were right about the overalls," she said to Ty, who automatically reached out to give her a hand getting off the tractor, then instantly released her once her feet were on the earthen barn floor.

"Coveralls," he corrected as he started walking toward the wide door they'd just driven through. Alvin leaped off the trailer and followed. The way he'd been guarding the thing, Madeline had wondered if Ty would have to coax the dog off.

"There's a difference?" she asked, catching up with him, which wasn't easy because of all the excess fabric she was dealing with.

"Overalls have straps, but no sleeves. Not as warm."

"I'll remember that. Do you wear overalls in the summer?"

He shot her a yeah-right look.

"Just curious." They stopped at the haystack, where the snow still showed evidence of Ty's collapse the previous day. He rolled back the tarp and used the hay hooks, which looked a lot like Captain Hook's prosthetic device, to pull two bales down. Then he cut the strings.

"Carry what you can to the manger and try to find an open spot to toss it in."

"Open spot?"

"You'll see what I mean when you get there." He stabbed the hooks back into the hay and left them hanging, then began to tie the tarp back down.

Madeline lifted an armload of hay. The bulls immediately crowded the feeder in a most intimidating way and, yes, she did understand now about a clear spot. As she stood uncertainly, trying to figure out how to throw the hay without it hitting an animal's head, Ty came up behind her and expertly tossed a few flakes over the fence and into the far end.

The bulls followed the hay and Madeline set her load in the closer, much less crowded end. "I see you need an arm for this."

"And height, to make it over the fence."

"You wouldn't be foolish enough to call me short, would you?"

He smiled, then seemed to remember himself. "I can feed the horses alone," he told her. "It's cold. Why don't you get on inside and warm up?"

"I'll go with you. I'd like to see Gabby." Skip's horse, which was her horse now.

Ty's gaze shifted. "Gabby's not here."

"Where is she?"

"I loaned her to a kid for a 4-H project. She's super gentle and the kid isn't all that comfortable with horses, so…" he shrugged "…I saw the want ad in the post office and offered Gabby. I probably should have contacted you first."

"That's fine. I'm glad she's being used."

They started walking side by side through the snow toward the horse corral and another stack of hay. Madeline slid on an icy patch in the snow and Ty reached out, but missed her as she went down. Snow trickled down her collar, bringing back childhood memories. Big hands hauled her up out of the snow, then Ty stepped back as she dusted herself off.

"I didn't recoil," he said solemnly. "You just went down too fast."

"Yeah, yeah." She started for the corral again and Ty fell into step. "You probably reached out, then quickly pulled your hands back." She caught his brief smile.

"What's that building there?" she asked, pointing to the shed with the padlock.

"Workshop," Ty replied shortly, making her think it was a sore spot.

"Why is it locked?" Madeline asked.

"There's stuff in there I don't want stolen."

"Without sounding...cold-blooded, is it your stuff or ranch stuff?"

"My stuff."

"I'm not trying to pry into your private affairs."

"I know." He didn't look at her, but instead moved ahead and started undoing the bungees that held the hay tarp in place. "And I'm not trying to be secretive. I used to make things out of silver. I haven't done it in a while."

"What kind of things?"

"Belt buckles. Spurs. Bits."

"Skip never said anything about that." But after he'd figured out that his family wasn't thrilled with his new occupation, he didn't communicate as many personal things with them as he once had. Another of her regrets.

"Too busy?"

"I don't feel like silversmithing right now." His tone was blunt, colder than before. His shields were going up.

He started carrying hay and tossing it over the fence.

There were only two horses, so Madeline stood back and let him do his job.

"Well, maybe one of these days."

"Yeah." He fastened the tarp in place. "I hear my lifestyle might be changing soon. Maybe I'll have more free time."

GOOD WAY TO THROW a bucket of ice water on a conversation that was actually working between the two of them. He had to stop allowing himself to be pulled in a direction he couldn't go.

"Yes. Maybe," Madeline replied. "Ty..." She seemed for once to be at a loss for words. Then she gave a small shake of her head and said, "I think I'll go back to my house. It's getting cold."

He watched her walk away, feeling regret mixed with relief. This had been his objective, breathing room, but it had been a while since he'd had an actual conversation with someone that wasn't related to cows and that lasted for more than a couple of minutes. He'd talked. She'd talked.

That was what people did. They had conversations. He'd been alone for so long that doing what was perfectly normal to others felt foreign to him.

How healthy was that?

He didn't know, didn't care. He'd survive. He seemed to have a knack for that.

He fed the cow in the barn, then headed out the door next to his former workshop, pausing before he passed it on his way to the equipment shed.

The padlock was encased in frost.

When was the last time he'd opened it?

TY DIDN'T SEE MADELINE for the rest of the morning. She stayed in her house; he tended to servicing the tractor. Alvin trotted toward the house when he was done, knowing the routine—chores, lunch and then paperwork. Ty wasn't up for writing grants, but the deadline was approaching fast.

He was just opening his back door when Sam turned into the driveway, pulling the vet truck up next to Madeline's car a few minutes later.

"I'm between calls and thought I'd see how the cow's doing." Sam indicated the little car with a jerk of his head. "I guess your partner made it back the other day?"

"Yes, she did," Ty said drily. The two men fell into step as they crossed the yard to the barn.

"Still driving you crazy?"

Ty nodded. He didn't want to go into it.

"How is she?" Sam asked. "The cow, I mean."

"The same."

"Too bad. She's a nice-looking animal." Sam reached down to pet Alvin while Ty unlatched the door.

Sam checked the cow over, then stood back. "Give her a little more time. I have enough medication in the truck for another week if you want."

"I want." He liked this cow.

Madeline was digging around in her trunk when Ty latched the barn door.

"I think you're about to meet my partner," he said.

"Mmm-hmm," Sam agreed.

Ty wondered if Madeline had thought about their conversation that morning as much as he had, and had come to the conclusion that he was a jerk, and decided to keep her distance. Not likely, knowing Madeline, but if she had, it would make things simpler.

She pulled out a tote bag and then pushed the trunk closed. She hadn't bothered with a jacket and the red sweater hugged her body, emphasizing the area that Ty had gotten a glimpse of after the mouse incident. The hair around her face was wavier than usual, making her appear soft, approachable. Appearances could be deceiving, Ty thought.

"Hi," she said to Sam before either guy could speak. "You must be the man who belongs to this truck." She smiled at Sam as if he was an old friend, and offered a hand. Ty blinked.

"Hi," Sam echoed, taking her extended hand briefly, and returning her smile in a way that made Ty want to remind him that he was happily married. "Sam Hyatt."

"Madeline Blaine. I'm Skip's sister."

"Nice to meet you." Sam's tone was both amused and sincere. Ty was struck by how he felt remarkably territorial.

What the hell?

"Sam's our vet," Ty said in a clipped voice. The red flags popping up in his brain didn't keep him from emphasizing the word *our*.

Madeline gave him a look, then turned back to Sam. "How's the cow?"

"If she doesn't start using her hindquarters in the next week, not good, I'm afraid."

"Do you hang many cows?"

Sam grinned crookedly. "Only the bad ones."

Madeline smiled at his poor joke, even though the subject wasn't all that funny. "I've got some things to attend to. Nice meeting you, Sam."

When Madeline disappeared into her house, tote bag in hand, Sam didn't say a word. Ty shifted his weight.

"Your partner is a nice-looking woman," Sam finally ventured.

Ty nodded.

"I'd better get going to my next call."

"Thanks for coming by." Ty shoved his hands into his pockets.

"No problem," Sam replied wryly. "See you in about a week."

ODDLY, MADELINE—who hated distractions of any kind while working—seemed to write very productively whenever Ty irritated her. This was the second time it had happened, and if she continued at this rate, she'd have the memoir done before she left.

Just thinking about him glowering at her, as if he wished she was anywhere but here, on the property she half owned, sent her fingers flying over the keys.

They'd had a decent morning, right up until he'd shut down. She could make allowances for the fact that she might trigger memories of Skip and the accident, but when she saw him later with the vet, it had felt like something else. As if he'd tried to fake civility that morning and had discovered he just couldn't do it, and he wasn't going to try any longer.

It felt personal.

It shouldn't bother you. She stabbed the save button and closed the chapter she'd finished.

But it did. A week ago it wouldn't have, but today... today it annoyed the heck out of her. He might be hurting, but she had to work with this guy. Be his partner. They needed some ground rules.

She worked through most of the afternoon, turning the generator off after lunch and switching over to longhand to save fuel. She felt a degree of satisfaction when she finally tidied her notes into a stack. Tonight she'd transcribe onto her netbook and email it to herself. No. Scratch that. She'd back up to a JumpDrive.

Being cut off from services she'd taken for granted up until now took some getting used to, but she was getting better. In a way it was relaxing to know she wasn't going to get interrupted by a call right when a brilliant thought struck her. Or that she wouldn't be tempted to call her lawyer, just because. She'd worked so hard to get to where she was that the thought of leaving in disgrace...

She had to quit thinking so much.

About an hour before dark, Madeline left her toasty-warm house to turn on the generator. The barn was quiet when she stepped inside. Ty wasn't there, so Madeline went to check on the patient before starting the noisy machine.

The cow turned her head and blinked as Madeline approached. The manger was empty, and the animal looked bored. Madeline dumped in another armload of hay and the cow plunged her nose in.

"You'd better start thinking positive healing thoughts," she said softly, reaching out to touch the animal's neck. The hair was more bristly than Madeline had expected. She brought her hand up to her nose. Her fingers smelled of warm, musky animal.

The door at the far end of the barn scraped open and Madeline stepped back from the cow, her pulse rate jumping. A few seconds later Ty came around the haystack, stopping when he saw her.

"I didn't know you were here," he said as he started toward the manger again. Madeline clenched her teeth at his flat, dismissive tone.

"I fed her," she said to his back. "I can do that. She's half mine, you know."

Ty turned. She stood, arms folded over her chest, her weight on one leg, and his hands dropped loosely to his sides in a resigned gesture. He obviously recognized a woman with something to say.

"Our relationship is complex," she began, stating the obvious.

"True," he said with no change in expression.

"I know your life is different since I've arrived, but the truth of the matter is that I could live here forever if I so chose."

Did he just go pale?

"You could," he allowed cautiously. "But you don't belong here, Maddie."

She shook her head, even though his statement was for all intents and purposes true. "No. You don't want me here. We've established that. But being short-tempered and glowering at me isn't going to make me leave. Maybe we'll never be friends, but we need a truce. A *full-time* truce."

Ty cocked his head. "Okay. I'm guilty of being short-tempered, but glowering?" he said, ignoring her last statement. "What the hell's that? Something I do after recoiling?"

"You know, like today when I was talking to the vet? And you wanted me to disappear to the other side of the planet?"

For a moment she thought he was going to disagree with her, but he didn't.

"Things have been different since you've been here," he admitted. "And we didn't start off well."

"I know," she said softly. "The accusations I made against you when I first came…I apologize. They were unfounded."

Ty regarded her silently. Madeline forged on. "But we have had a few friendly moments. I would really like it if we could have more and maintain a civil relationship… without the aid of Amuma. For the business partnership, if nothing else."

Ty glanced over her shoulder at the cow behind her, as if looking for a hint from the animal. "You're right."

He spoke without emotion even though his gaze was intent. "We can maintain a civil relationship. For the sake of the partnership. Without wine." He shifted his weight slightly and added, "And I'll accept your apology, if you accept mine."

She held out a hand in way of an answer, and he took it, his fingers warm and firm on hers. His touch felt as good as she'd thought it would.

The pressure of his fingers increased before he let go. She instantly missed the warmth of his weather-roughened skin on hers. Ty looked at the cow again, then back at her, giving the impression of a man who needed to escape.

He cleared his throat. "Since you have everything covered here, I guess I'll go back to my place." He pushed his hands into his pockets.

"Me, too," Madeline said, following the movement of his hands before bringing her eyes back up to his. "My place, I mean."

"I knew what you meant."

But he sounded relieved.

TALK ABOUT MISREADING a situation... He supposed he should be thankful that Madeline thought he'd been glowering, as she called it, because the truth was he'd felt like punching out his vet. And he needed the guy.

He went into his house and turned off the generator, then made his way unerringly to his bedroom without a flashlight. Three years of practice had taught him never to leave anything lying in the path.

What was happening to him? Was he falling for Skip's sister in spite of everything? What else explained the protectiveness, or the desire to tell Sam to step off, even when he knew Sam was devoted to his wife?

Ty couldn't fall for Madeline. Not now.

No apology on earth was going to make up for what he'd done. Especially when she didn't know the entire truth. All she had was the cop report. She didn't know how much he had to apologize for.

And he didn't know if he could tell her.

CHAPTER FOURTEEN

NOBODY HAD PREDICTED the snowstorm. It slipped down from the north during the night and dumped at least eight inches. Ty woke to a winter wonderland, a head-ache and a pasture full of hungry livestock.

He wanted to get them fed before Madeline showed up to help.

"We'll do this alone, okay?" he muttered to Alvin, who was watching him put on his boots at least an hour earlier than usual. "It's nasty out there."

Alvin whimpered. In answer? Or in protest for chang-ing the routine? Border collies loved their routines.

Ty didn't bother to turn off the generator when he let himself out into the early-morning darkness. He had to chain up the tractor so he could plow a path to the haystack and then to the field.

The barn was dark, since Madeline's generator, which powered the lights for the barn the rare occasions that he needed them, wasn't on. He propped his flashlight on the ground and then shook out the chains and laid them out.

Would Madeline hear the tractor and think he was ditching her? Would she understand that he just needed to be alone? For real this time. He'd had not one, but two nightmares the night before, something that hadn't happened since the weeks following the wreck.

How great was that? Just thinking about confessing had given him nightmares.

Ty opened the door to vent the exhaust fumes, then started the tractor and backed it over the chains. It took only a few minutes to secure them around the tires and then he got into the driver's seat and pulled out of the barn, dropping the blade as soon as he cleared the door.

The snow was heavy and wet. When it froze it was going to be icy as hell. And he was almost out of food. He'd planned to take a run to town that day, but now he wasn't so sure.

His other choice, though, was to remain marooned on the ranch with Madeline, perhaps even dependent on her to eat.

He'd take his chances on the road.

TY WAS IN THE FIELD feeding when Madeline let herself out of the house. It was still dark and the tractor headlights cast long yellow beams over the pasture. The snow on the porch was almost over her boot tops, but she had no choice but to step out into it as she started pushing it off the steps. She gave up on the idea of shoveling any kind of a path. Where would she shovel to?

She went back inside, put on Ty's coveralls, pulling them down over her boots so the snow wouldn't get in. The tractor had woken her up, and it hadn't been too hard to figure out that the only reason Ty would be setting out much earlier than usual was so that he could do the chores alone.

She'd stayed in the sleeping bag, listening to the sounds of him plowing, until she couldn't take it anymore and had gotten up to make coffee. If Ty wanted to feed alone, that was his business.

But logical or not, she felt kind of abandoned.

She waded through the snow to where the bulls were pressing their intimidating bulk against the fence. Some were standing in the snowy trough, trying to get to the food she hadn't even uncovered yet. The fence creaked and Madeline worked faster. If Skip could do this ranch stuff, in all types of weather, so could she. She was here to understand.

The lifestyle? Or the man who was now her partner?

The two were tied together. Maybe she wanted an insight on both.

The tarp was heavy with new wet snow and hard to move, but she managed to loosen a corner and shake off enough that she could access the two bales she needed. She cut the strings with the pink beribboned knife Ty had left in the stack and then grabbed a small armload. The bulls pressed harder. She assumed a wide stance, looked for an open spot and threw the hay. They knocked it right back on top of her with their heads, volleyball style, in their effort to crowd one another out. She got another armload and moved closer, faked left, then awkwardly threw to the right. The bulls fell for it; the hay went over the fence and she got one or two distracted. She tried the same technique again, only this time reversing it. Score. Now that they were all busy eating she could fill the rest of the manger.

Once the bulls were fed, she tended to the much easier horses, then trudged back through the snow to the barn, where she turned on the generator.

Madeline let out the breath she'd been holding when it didn't explode or anything, and then went back behind the straw stack to where the poor cow hung. The animal looked up soulfully with her soft brown eyes.

"I hear you're a good producer," Madeline said. "And I happen to know that it's in your best interest to become a good producer again, so…well…you might want to get your feet back under you ASAP. Start producing."

Dear heavens, she was talking to a cow.

She fed her, then cleaned the pen, and when she was done felt a mild sense of accomplishment. She might not have been out driving the tractor, with the rush of cool air in her face, but she'd done her part.

Once again she patted the cow, which was busy eating and ignored her. But she shifted her rear end slightly. Madeline felt a small ray of hope. She'd kind of bonded with Sling Cow and wanted to see her walking around under her own steam.

Ty was driving in from the field when Madeline left the barn. She didn't bother waiting for him, but retreated to the warmth of her house.

SHE'D FED THE BULLS. Ty closed his eyes for a moment, kicking himself for not saying something the day before.

Then he walked straight to her house, climbed the steps and knocked on the door. It took her a few minutes to answer, and when she did, it was fairly obvious that she'd showered, but had not yet done whatever it was she did to her hair. The wet locks made her skin look even fairer than usual, her dark-lashed eyes greener. He stepped inside so she could close the door.

"Maddie—don't feed the bulls when I'm not here." She opened her mouth to speak, then saw something in his expression that made her close it again. "The big one has been known to come right over the top of the fence when he gets the urge. It's different if Alvin is there, but without him…" The bull had come through the fence only twice in the past two years, but both times it had been in deep snow when he was hungry. It would have killed Ty if something had happened to Madeline.

"I didn't know."

One corner of his mouth tightened. "Because I didn't tell you." He never dreamed she would take on feeding chores on her own. "I'm sorry."

"Lots to this ranching game that I've yet to learn," she said with forced lightness.

"Yeah. There is." He reached out to touch her cheek with his gloved hand, then instantly wished he hadn't. But he had, and Madeline's lips parted slightly as he let his arm fall back down to his side. "I, uh, just wanted to tell you."

And now he needed to leave instead of staring down into her very green eyes, wide with…what? They hadn't widened until he'd touched her.

"I'll see you later." He turned and opened the door before she could answer, then closed it quietly behind him. When he got to his own door, his stomach was still in a tight knot.

Ty spent the morning on the grant, since he had a headache anyway, and it kept him from thinking about Madeline. The phone rang shortly after ten, startling him. Only a handful of people called him on that line. Hell, since he'd backed off from social contact over the past two years, pretty much no one called unless it was business related.

"Hello, Ty. This is Susan at the post office."

"Hi, Susan," Ty said with a sense of foreboding.

"Madeline received an official-looking letter. I thought she might want to get it once the roads are clear."

"I'll pass the message along." Although there was no way her little car was going to make it to the gate, much less to town with the new accumulation of snow.

"And you have that package I'm sure she told you about. Things are getting crowded down here. You really need to pick it up."

"Okay." Madeline hadn't mentioned a package, but she probably thought he collected his mail regularly, like a normal person. And he had, until she'd showed up. After that he'd stayed on the ranch, almost as if he was guarding it from her.

"Would you happen to remember who the package was from?" Ty asked. Susan remembered everything, from the tiniest gossip to the person who had sent the nicest valentine in the fourth grade.

"Your mother, Ty. You might want to get this one."

"Thanks, Susan. I'll be down today or tomorrow depending on the roads."

"Have a good day, Ty. Goodbye."

She'd already hung up by the time he said goodbye back.

His mom had sent him a package. At Christmas. They emailed regularly and she knew what a hard time this was for him, even if he didn't spell it out. So why would she have sent him a gift?

Keep an open mind, he reminded himself, remembering how Madeline had insisted she was doing that concerning the ranch.

Open minds took a hell of a lot of willpower.

MADELINE WAS GETTING nowhere on her book when Ty knocked on her door. The power was off, so no issues there. Maybe he needed help with something. She dropped her pen onto the legal pad and answered the door.

"Susan from the post office called. You have an official-looking letter. I think that means you have to sign for it."

Madeline's stomach tightened. An official letter could be good news…but what were the chances?

"I could probably sign as your agent."

Her eyes shot up to his. "You're going to town?"

"Either that or starve."

"Can I ride along?"

"As long as you know the risks. I can't guarantee safe passage down the mountain and back up again. We may end up stuck and walking."

She considered the matter for a few seconds—or pretended to. She wanted that letter. Madeline had never been a big one for surprises. "I'll wear the coveralls if I have to."

A slight smile briefly curved his mouth. Someday she was going to have to see if she could coax another real smile out of him.

As soon as Ty left, she changed into her jeans. In a way, Nevada had been very good for her, since life on the ranch had lessened her professional anxiety. During the day she was fully able to believe Everett's assertions that he had legal matters firmly in hand and she had nothing to worry about. At night...well, at night she still tended to obsess. But she had to put her faith in her lawyer. She was, after all, innocent, and this was, after all, a formality. The legal department covering all bases.

So what was this official letter?

She slipped into her boots.

Madeline bit her lip. She wasn't going to think about it until she had the letter in her hand, because obsessing about it on the drive down the mountain wouldn't help.

ACTUALLY, TY HAD ENOUGH food to make it a couple more days if he didn't mind diving into the emergency canned goods, and he had to post the grant application day after tomorrow, so he'd be making another trip to town then. But Madeline wanted this letter. If their positions were reversed and his professional future was in question, he'd probably drive through deep snow to get an official letter, so that was exactly what he was going to do for Madeline. He owed her.

When he started the truck, she came out of her trailer, and damned if she wasn't carrying the coveralls. She wore her puffy coat and sissy gloves, and a giant scarf was draped over her shoulders, almost dragging on the ground.

"Where's your beret?" Ty asked as she got into the rig.

"In my pocket."

"Heck of a scarf you have there," he said when she shut the thing in the door and had to open the door again to pull it out. He wanted to keep things normal. No glowering. No reason for Madeline to come at him again. He'd be the civil business partner that he'd promised her he'd try to be.

"My grandmother made it for me," she said. "Grandma always was an overachiever." The look she gave him came across as self-conscious. He had the strong impression that she, too, was trying hard to act normal. Great. They could both fake normal during what would undoubtedly be a long trip to town.

Ty put the truck in gear and drove to the gate. He'd plowed to the county road, but after that it was a matter of four-wheel drive and silent prayers.

"Where does your grandmother live?" he asked, his eyes on the road. He'd left the gate open so he wouldn't have to stop.

"In a retirement community for the academic crowd."

"I've never heard of such a thing."

"Well, you know how some retirement communities are built around golf courses? This one is built around a library and computer labs. Most of the people there taught at some level. There are a few researchers, though."

Ty shook his head. "What did your grandmother teach? Or was she a researcher?"

"She taught. She was in anthropology."

"Is that why you went into it?"

"Pretty much. My grandfather was a brilliant businessman, so he paid the bills and Grandma bent young minds. Skip took after him and I took after her."

"I see." He didn't want to talk about Skip.

"Nobody understood why Skip abandoned his MBA studies to become a rancher."

"He loved it," Ty said shortly.

"So I hear."

The truck was handling the deep snow well, but he focused on the road with more intensity than necessary, hoping Madeline would change the subject. No such luck.

"I told him he was a fool for doing what he did— sinking Grandpa's inheritance into the ranch."

"I can see your point," Ty said stonily. Did she think

that by talking about Skip it would help desensitize him? Fat chance.

After a few minutes of unexpected silence, Ty shot a look her way. She stared straight ahead out the windshield, lost in thought, and all Ty could think was *I killed your brother.*

The wheels hit a rut, dragging the truck toward the ditch, and Ty fought to keep it on the road. He managed. Barely.

"Well done," Madeline murmured. She hadn't so much as put a hand down to balance herself.

"Thanks," he said automatically. "What do your parents do?" he blurted apropos of nothing.

"Gallivant."

"Excuse me?"

Madeline smiled. It was possible she was thinking about the letter and not her brother. He was the one fixated on Skip. "They divorced when I was ten and Skip was eight. Skip and I moved in with our grandparents while they worked out custody, and we never left. I guess they never quite got custody hammered out."

"You aren't close to them?"

"We're in sporadic contact. How about you?"

"My mom lives in Arizona, where I grew up. She married a nice guy there and has lived near Phoenix for almost twenty years."

"Your parents are divorced?"

"Never married, but they did have a custody deal. I saw my dad during all the holidays, summers. I loved this area, which is where he lived at the time, so that's why I bought here."

"Where's he now?"

Ty gave her a sidelong look, noting the concern in her face. "Sacramento. He married an urbanite who refuses to live outside the city limits."

"Do you see him?"

"Not as much as I used to, but yeah. I see him." His dad had used his vacation time to come to the ranch to help out for the first weeks after the accident, but phones calls were few and far between. Ty and his dad understood each other. He remembered the package at the post office. He'd thought his mother understood, too.

The drive off the mountain went better than Ty had anticipated. Only two close calls. Madeline hadn't had to put on the coveralls and she had told him about her teaching job, which she seemed to like and was half afraid she might lose. Her face had clouded as she talked about it, making him want to punch out this Jensen asshole.

As they drove past the school, a draft horse pulling a wagon loaded with hay and kids crossed the intersection ahead of them. Madeline leaned forward in her seat.

"Look at that!"

Behind the horse and wagon came McKirk's antique International pickup truck with more hay and a bunch of adults.

Great. The Christmas parade. He'd gone every year when he was a kid.

"What's going on?" Madeline asked as what appeared to be the rest of the town trooped by on foot, talking and laughing.

"Christmas parade."

"Wow. If everyone in town participates, that doesn't leave many spectators."

"Us."

"Where are they going?"

"The park. I think they have drinks and stuff there. I haven't been to one of these since I was twelve or thirteen."

He could see that Madeline wanted to follow the action. Instead, after the last of the parade passed by, he turned onto the main street and drove to the post office. She didn't say a word.

Ty held the door open for her and she preceded him into the building. A whiff of potpourri hit his nostrils. Garlands were hung around the ceiling and he quickly looked for mistletoe. To avoid it. He could easily see Susan demanding a kiss.

The postmistress beamed at them. "It's good to see you two. You just missed the parade."

"No, we saw it," Madeline said with a smile. Susan handed her the envelope and had her sign at least three cards. Madeline's hands shook a little as she ripped into the envelope and pulled out a single sheet of paper, which she scanned.

Ty wanted to ask if it was bad news, but kept his mouth shut. Madeline finally nodded, then refolded the paper.

"Just the formal summons to the hearing," she said. "Rather than an informal hearing of inquiry, they've decided to initiate a full procedure."

"Which is?"

"Inquiry committee hearing followed by investigative committee hearing."

"Here's your package, Ty." Susan hefted a brown-paper-wrapped parcel onto the counter.

"Nothing to sign?" he asked as he took it.

"It's yours free and clear," Susan said with a laugh. "Enjoy."

"I hope," Ty muttered. Madeline, distracted, was already on her way out.

"Goodbye," she called to Susan at the last minute. Ty gave the postmistress a nod and headed after Madeline, his package under one arm.

"What now?" he asked as the door closed behind them. He'd never seen so much uncertainty in her expression before.

"I don't know. I'll have to make some phone calls."

"You can make them from the café. Have a cup of coffee and then we can shop."

"Are you sure the café is open?" she asked, indicating the tracks in the snow from the parade.

"I'm sure."

CHAPTER FIFTEEN

THE CAFÉ WAS OPEN, but no one appeared to be inside.

"They forgot to lock the door," Madeline whispered to Ty.

"I don't think they'll hear you," he replied in a normal voice that seemed overly loud in the deserted room. He leaned over the counter, craning his neck to see into the back room. "Hello…?"

His voice echoed into the kitchen. He waited a minute, then grabbed the coffeepot and two mugs.

"Are you allowed to do that?" Madeline asked as she took a seat at the nearest table and he began to pour.

"I don't see anyone here to stop me. Want pie or anything?" he asked, still holding the pot.

"Uh…no." Madeline peeled the top off a creamer and dumped it into her coffee. She liked to think of herself as fearless, but she didn't often break rules—and right now, with the new development in her case, she wasn't feeling nearly as fearless as usual.

"You need to make your phone calls?"

"Eventually," she said. She'd already checked for messages. Nothing from Everett, and an apology from Connor for not answering her call. He'd lost his phone and it had taken him a day to find it. And this was the guy in charge of recording grades for her classes.

They drank their coffee in silence, but it wasn't an uncomfortable one. Every now and then Ty would glance at the box he'd set on the table beside them, frown and then look back at his coffee. Or at her, but those looks were fleeting, as if he was distracted.

"Is the package something you were expecting?" Madeline finally asked.

"I can honestly say no."

He didn't expand on the answer and Madeline didn't ask any more questions. When he finished his coffee, he took his cup to the counter. "I'll step outside if you want to make your calls."

"You don't have to," she said, taking her phone out of her purse. She wasn't going to discuss anything too private. She hoped.

"I haven't heard anything," Connor said when she called. "People are being quiet and I can't exactly ask them what they know."

"No," Madeline agreed. Ty was near the door, leaning one shoulder against the wall as he read last week's newspaper, giving her some privacy.

"Are you still coming back on the twenty-third? Or sooner?"

Madeline inhaled deeply. "I'll talk to Everett."

"Come back on the twenty-third," Connor advised. "You'll only go nuts here. And since you can't work at the college, what will you do?"

"Visit my grandmother, who, by the way, figured everything out."

"No!" Connor groaned. "It wasn't me. I deflected her questions."

"Body language, Connor. You have to work on your body language."

"I didn't—" He broke off with the same sputter that had told Eileen something was up.

"Never mind. We had a long talk. I'm to learn about the ranching business before I come home."

"Good way to keep your mind occupied."

Madeline glanced over at Ty, letting her gaze run down to his boots, then back up to his dark head. "Yeah," she said with a slight frown. "Exactly."

She dialed Everett next. "I halfway expected this," he told her, shortly after saying hello. "I think the college will want to muddy the waters as much as possible to protect Jensen, allow him to keep that huge chunk of grant funding, as well as future grant funding. But…" he paused for lawyerly emphasis "…this will have no effect on the outcome of the case."

"You're sure? Or are you trying to stop me from flying across the country and camping in your office?"

"Both. Have some faith, Madeline. This is just more mental flogging from Dr. Mann. A power play."

"You're right." And in a weird way that made Madeline feel better. All part of the process.

As soon as she set her phone on the table, Ty came back over. "Everything okay?"

She nodded slowly. "According to my lawyer this was to be expected." She shrugged philosophically.

"You've never been in trouble before, have you?"

Madeline smiled slightly. "Not really."

"I was probably in enough trouble for both of us when I was a kid."

"You were a bad boy?" She tried to imagine Ty being bad. It wasn't that difficult, since there was more to him than he let show, and he was serving her coffee that didn't belong to him.

"An unsupervised boy, since Mom was working nights back then. But...I didn't do anything other than normal kid stuff."

"I didn't even do that. Skip did, but I didn't." His face went blank at the mention of her brother's name, as it always did.

Should she tell him that talking about Skip kept him alive in her heart? Suggest he try it?

One look at Ty's closed-off expression gave her the answer to that question. No.

They put their cups on the counter, Ty slipped the five-dollar bill under one of them, then they got in the truck and drove the two blocks to the mercantile. Anne was at her post.

"Why aren't you two at the park?" she demanded.

"We have other things to do," Ty said easily. "How are you, Anne?"

The woman's expression unexpectedly softened. "Not bad," she muttered. "Yourself?"

Ty gave the woman that fleeting smile Madeline kind of wished she saw more of. "Hanging in."

"You?" Anne said curtly to Madeline, who felt like a deer in the headlights.

"Uh, well. I'm doing well."

Anne nodded and sat back down on her stool next to the cash register. She had a game of solitaire spread out on the shelf under the checkout counter. She waved a hand.

"You two better get your shopping done. I'm closing in half an hour to join in the festivities."

Ty took a plastic basket off the stack and handed another to Madeline. She ended up filling two baskets while Ty filled five. It had apparently been a while since he'd been to a grocery store. Or anywhere, for that matter. To her knowledge, he'd left the ranch only once while she'd been there.

They loaded their purchases in the back of the extended cab and Alvin happily jumped into the truck bed.

"Won't he get cold?" Madeline asked.

"No colder than he'd get feeding."

"Good point."

As they pulled out of town, Madeline cast a wistful look toward several antique automobiles and two horse-drawn wagons in the park. There was a fire in the barbecue pit and people milled around holding drinks.

Ty briefly considered stopping, but when he saw folks starting to take their places on the homemade risers, he gave the truck some gas. No Christmas carols. Maybe in a year or two, but right now, with Skip's sister next to him…no. All he needed was to wig out while she was there.

Madeline didn't say a word, which made him feel even worse. But it wasn't as if he could just drop her off at the park and pick her up again later. The sky was growing gray and another snowstorm was predicted for tonight. He needed to get home, take care of the cow, work on the grant.

And Madeline would do what?

Write her book, probably. How did she keep from going stir-crazy in that house all alone? Skip had had about a million things going on—calculating budgets, reading books on ranching techniques, learning to silversmith.

His half-finished spurs were still in the shed. Ty should give them to Madeline. He hadn't known if she could handle it before, but she was dealing with grief a lot better than he was. Probably because her grief wasn't tainted with guilt.

"You wanted to go to that Christmas party in the park, didn't you?" He waited until he'd turned into the driveway before asking the question. It was the first words spoken during the entire forty-minute drive.

"I wanted to see what it was about."

Ty pulled the truck to a stop, then half turned in his seat.

"How about I make it up to you?" he heard himself ask.

Stop now.

"How?" she asked.

Alarm bells continued to go off in his head, but unable to stop himself, he pressed on. "I'll cook you some dinner."

"Real non-microwave food?"

"I didn't say that."

Madeline laughed. He liked her laugh. It was husky, and the few times he'd heard it, it had taken him by surprise. Maybe because she was so uptight and serious most of the time that when she let go it drove home the point that there was another side of her.

"What time?"

"Six?" That would give him a few hours to regret giving in to himself.

"I'll be there," Madeline said, reaching for the door handle. She jumped out into the deep snow and started pulling her bags out of the back. Ty helped her, so it took only one trip.

"No longer locking the door?" he said when she twisted the knob and let them into the trailer.

She gave him a sidelong look. "I've gotten to where I trust my neighbors."

TY'S HAIR WAS STILL DAMP from the shower when Madeline knocked on his back door, but he was dressed and ready to cook. It was the first time he'd cooked for anyone since Skip had died, and he was trying hard not to think about that.

Madeline took off her coat and draped it over the sofa.

He pointed to a cabinet. "I have some wine if you want to pick out a bottle. Or there's beer in the fridge."

"Wine?" Madeline arched an eyebrow.

"No Amuma," he said as he tore lettuce into a bowl. "Just regular old house wine."

"In that case, I'll take a chance on the wine."

Madeline opened the cupboard and pulled out a bottle of Spanish red.

"Glasses are over the stove."

"Got a ladder?"

"I'll get them as soon as I'm done with this," he said.

Madeline ignored him and dragged a kitchen chair over to the stove and stood on it. "I'm kind of used to this," she said. "Five foot two is a nice height to sing about, but a bit unhandy in the real world."

"Five foot two, eyes of green?" Ty asked, as he finished dicing a tomato.

"I know. Doesn't have the same ring as eyes of blue."

"I like green eyes," he said offhandedly. He was trying to be civil, but was edging into man-woman territory and needed to take a step back.

"Yeah?" Madeline asked as she stabbed the corkscrew into the top of the bottle.

"I'll do that," he said, dropping the knife and stepping closer.

"I can do it." Madeline started working the cork out, a pout of concentration on her face as she turned the mechanism.

"Have at it." He went to the oven.

"Smells good. Somehow I thought we'd have the classic guy meal."

"Which is?"

"Steak, potatoes and salad."

"We were this close," he said, holding up his thumb and forefinger, "but all the steaks are frozen rock-hard and I hate defrosting them in the microwave. Destroys the texture."

"And this is real lasagna?" she asked, pouring two jars of wine and then handing him one.

"Real as it gets…while still coming out of a box. But it isn't in the microwave," he said, gesturing to the oven.

"I would have settled for microwave food just to have a chance to eat somewhere other than in that trailer."

"Lonely over there?" Of course it had to be lonely. He was used to this life. She wasn't. But it wasn't as if he hadn't warned her.

"The place is a little stark."

"I would think that all that starkness would be good for writing. No distractions."

"It's much better now that the ink in my pen is no longer freezing solid."

She smiled at him over her glass. The same smile she'd smiled when she'd gunned the tractor, nearly knocking him off.

"I hear there's a special ink antifreeze additive that will solve that problem if you ever run out of wood."

Her smile widened, lighting her eyes. "I'll have to

look into it." She sipped the wine she'd been swirling in her glass. "Not the same as Amuma."

"No," Ty agreed. "This wine doesn't sneak up and knock you on your ass."

The timer dinged and he took the lasagna out of the oven.

"Are you going to let it sit?"

"Nope." Using a spatula, he started dividing portions.

"I'll get the salad."

It had been more than two years since Ty had shared a table with a woman, but he hadn't forgotten how to go through the motions, refilling her glass, smiling when she said something funny—and Madeline could be surprisingly amusing.

"How was Sling Cow tonight?" she asked after he'd cleared the table. He was going to have to shoo her on home soon, before he did something stupid and dangerous, such as suggesting that they settle in for a movie on DVD.

"I think she's improving. We'll know tomorrow when Sam stops by." *Who is married, by the way.* "I called him to come and take a look."

Madeline swirled more than she drank, Ty noticed, and he vowed to do the same. He wanted to avoid loose lips, although he couldn't exactly blame the wine for telling her she had nice eyes earlier, since he hadn't had a drop at that time.

For a moment there, he'd forgotten the circumstances. Lonely guy. Attractive woman. Dinner. Etc.

Except that tonight held no etc. for him. Or her.

They would both do without, although he had to admit he was getting something out of the edgy feeling she gave him, and had a dangerous urge to surrender to it and push a little. See how Madeline would respond.

And then the guilt would smack him back.

If she'd been there under different circumstances, related to anyone else...

"What happens when you go back home?" he asked abruptly. The smile faded from her eyes. "I mean concerning your job. You have the hearing and then what?"

"After the inquiry hearing, there will be an investigative hearing. I was hoping to skip that step, but Everett, my lawyer, says it was inevitable. I only hope I can teach my spring classes. Everett says I shouldn't worry."

"But you still do."

"Of course I do," she said. "I've worked hard to get where I am."

Ty leaned back in his chair. "Can you tell me what happened? The articles were sketchy."

"Not much to tell really." She poured another glass of wine and offered the bottle to Ty. He shook his head. Best to keep his wits about him.

"There's a small isolated group of indigenous people in northern Canada. They gave blood samples to the university for tests. Very specific tests involving certain diseases. Dr. Jensen—and I don't know how he got access—used some of the samples for other studies."

"And that's bad?"

"It is if the tribe didn't give permission for that usage. Giving blood doesn't mean it can be tested for just anything. Plus...Jensen discovered links to northern European races that counter the tribe's traditional beliefs about their origins. He was very excited. They were not."

"So it's a big deal?"

"It could affect federal funding to the college. He shouldn't have had the samples, shouldn't have used them without permission."

"How long ago did this happen?"

"He did the work two years ago. I got my position as associate professor a year and half ago, so I was still his assistant."

"And the situation is just coming to light."

"The work just got published. I don't think he believed the tribe would notice, but he was wrong. It caused an uproar."

"Did you suspect at all?"

Madeline's chin went up as she regarded him through slightly narrowed eyes. "What do you think?"

"I think you're the original Goody Two-Shoes, which is why you were so nervous about drinking coffee today without permission."

"It showed?"

"It showed." He felt himself getting sucked in again, wanting to respond to her in a way that he didn't think his dead partner would approve of. Ty really wanted to reach out and touch her face, see what that silky dark hair felt like as it slid through his fingers. It'd been so long since he'd been with a woman, or even felt the warmth of connecting with someone. Why this woman?

"Why don't I cook for you tomorrow?" she asked out of the blue, the husky note in her voice telling him that she felt the same connection he did, perhaps even had the same questions. "And I can even make non-microwave food."

He really liked the idea, which was why he had to put the brakes on now.

He shook his head gently.

She tilted her head. "Because you don't like the way things are between us?" Trust Madeline to come right out and say it.

"No. I like having a civil relationship."

"Civil." She was obviously less than pleased at his word choice, even though civil was what she'd wanted earlier. A civil working relationship. "Doesn't this feel just a little more intimate than civil?"

His heart gave a mighty thud at the prospect. "I think, given the circumstances, maybe we'll keep our relationship right about where it is."

"What circumstances?"

He wasn't going to spell it out. "You know what circumstances."

She frowned slightly. "Did you get counseling after the accident?"

"No."

"You might consider it," she said matter-of-factly, rising from her chair and walking past him to collect her coat from the sofa.

"Can a counselor change the past, Madeline?"

She put on her coat. "No. But he or she might be able to help you deal with it."

"I'm not pouring my guts out to someone else when I know what the problem is. I killed your brother and I have to live with it."

He expected Madeline to draw back at his bald statement. Instead she studied him impassively for a few seconds before she said, "You didn't kill Skip. I read the report." Frustration crossed her face. "You have to deal with this, Ty. It doesn't get better on its own."

"I was there, Madeline. I know what happened. And maybe I'm not ready to get better."

She held his eyes for a moment, as if she couldn't quite believe what she'd heard, then draped her scarf over her shoulders, for once with nothing else to say. Ty went to open the door for her as she pulled on her gloves, having never successfully beaten down the manners his mother had instilled in him. Madeline glanced up, pausing in the doorway and letting in a swirl of frigid air. Ty was about to speak when she rose up on tiptoe and pressed her soft lips to the underside of his jaw, the highest point she could reach.

He felt the kiss down to his toes. Two seconds later she was gone and Ty closed the door, wondering what the hell had just happened.

THE PATH LEADING BACK to her house was dark, the air frigid, but Madeline didn't hurry. She walked slowly, the beam from her flashlight reflecting off the crystallized snow, creating tiny spectrums of light as she crunched along.

Okay, this was frustrating in the extreme. She was attracted to Ty. She'd danced around the issue for a while, indulged in denial, but there was no getting past it—she was attracted. And unless she'd misread him, Ty was attracted to her. When a man stared across the table at a woman the way Ty had been at her, and when that woman got butterflies in her stomach when she met that stare, something was going on.

Something he was not going to pursue because he hadn't dealt with his grief.

He liked being civil. Her lip curled slightly. So did she. But she rarely felt a connection to people she was simply civil to. She rarely kissed them, even on the jaw.

Damn it, Ty. I only want to be friends. Help you through this…thing…you've yet to deal with.

Madeline clunked up the wooden steps, cursing and then wondering why she cursed so much since crossing the Mississippi. Perhaps because she'd spent more time out of her comfort zone than she had in her entire life. They had a bond, because of what had happened, because they shared a life with Skip. She should help Ty. She wanted to help him.

She opened the door to her lonely, dark house and stepped inside without even automatically reaching for a light switch as she had when she'd first arrived. She stoked the stove by flashlight, then went to sit on her sofa bed. So could she convince him to let her help?

Not without a struggle. Maybe not at all. She might have to accept the situation as it was.

CHAPTER SIXTEEN

TY WASN'T SURPRISED when Madeline showed up the next morning to drive the tractor, since she wasn't the type to sidestep an awkward situation. And he didn't protest that his knee was better, even though it was. They needed to get past what had happened the night before—hopefully without talking about it.

He wondered if that was going to happen, especially since she'd brought up the subject of counseling. He really hoped she didn't bring it up again.

Just thinking about it froze him inside. Granted, some people benefited from talking to others. He wasn't one of them. Talking was simply another way of reliving the event, and he did that on a regular basis. Why have a witness to his pain?

He'd talked himself through what had happened more than once, coldly, clinically. No matter what excuse he gave himself, one hard fact remained. Skip had wanted to stop for the night; Ty had insisted they press on. If he hadn't been asleep at the wheel, then he'd been damned close when the cow had stepped out into the road, startling him so he'd overreacted and flipped the truck. The "almost asleep" part wasn't in the report that Madeline had read.

Skip was dead and Ty was panting after his sister. That seemed wrong on so many levels.

Madeline's clutch work was jerkier than usual that morning, but Ty braced himself and they fed without exchanging more than a couple words, which only amplified the awkwardness between them. He was even more aware of her than he'd been the night before.

After parking the tractor, Madeline went with him to care for Sling Cow, as she called the animal, and then headed back to her trailer without so much as a goodbye.

"Hey, Madeline." He couldn't help himself. He had to make her feel better.

She turned back.

"I'm sorry about last night. The way it ended."

She shrugged with exaggerated nonchalance. "No worries."

He took a few steps toward her, wondering why he hated seeing her walk away when it made perfect sense for them to go to their neutral corners. "I overreacted."

"I shouldn't have asked such personal questions."

He nodded, not knowing what else to do. "I'm going to replace a belt on your generator, so you won't have power for a little while. Is that okay?"

"Fine. Just give me time to shower. I'm going to town."

"We went to town yesterday."

"I have some personal matters to take care of."

"Be careful on the roads." He nodded again, feeling like a bobblehead, and headed for the generator.

THE ROAD DOWN the mountain had been plowed, so Madeline had no trouble making it to the mercantile, despite concentrating more on Ty than on driving.

After arguing with herself several times that morning, she'd given in and worked with him because she wanted to make a point—that they could move past the awkward way they'd parted the night before, and he didn't need to withdraw behind his icy wall. She'd achieved what she wanted. He had addressed the issue, they had some closure and could move on. Civilly.

And now, point made, Madeline needed to get off the ranch and away from him, where she could think more clearly. She still wanted to help him through his issues. It almost felt as if it was her duty, being Skip's sister.

She parked in front of the store and went inside, saying hello to Anne, who seemed surprised to see her back again this soon. Then Madeline grabbed a basket and disappeared down the first aisle. She didn't really need anything. Maybe more cereal, which she kept in the refrigerator after the mouse incident. She was eating a lot of cereal lately, since she could eat it without having power, and it seemed possible that she'd lost a few pounds. Her jeans were getting looser. Or maybe it was all that hay tossing. Or lack of sleep.

She stopped at the rotating book rack, reading the back covers. Usually she downloaded her books, but given her current sporadic electricity, paper and print were the best option. She continued to wander the aisles, killing time, guessing at the purpose of certain items. She reached for what looked like an odd kitchen device and held it at an angle, studying it.

"Hoof pick," Anne called across the store.

"Don't need one of those," Madeline called back. She headed to the counter with her basket of non-essentials.

"How much longer are you going to be here?" Anne asked as she rang up the purchases.

"A little over a week."

"Then you'll be heading back East for that hearing thing?"

Madeline stared at the older woman. How did she know? Surely Ty hadn't…

Anne jerked her head toward her small computer screen. "Do you look up everyone who comes through town?" Madeline asked with a frown. It was kind of creepy if she did.

"Pretty much. Nice to know who's doing what. We've had our share of criminals. Small places like this attract people who want to fall off the end of the earth."

Madeline placed both palms flat on the counter and leaned forward. "*I'm* not a criminal or trying to fall off the ends of the earth."

Anne lifted her eyes from the price tag she was trying to read without glasses. "Never said you were."

"I'm just guilty by association," Madeline added stiffly.

"Should pick your associates more carefully," the

shopkeeper said as she keyed the wrong price into the machine. Madeline didn't correct her. It was only twenty cents. But it was tempting to point out that Anne's glasses, which she probably thought she'd lost, were on top of her head. Madeline decided not to risk it.

"Amen to that," she murmured instead. She really couldn't blame Anne for looking her up. Not much to do in this store except play solitaire and watch TV. The internet had opened a whole new way to poke a nose into other people's business.

"Think you'll get off?"

"I do." Madeline pulled two twenties out of her pocket and handed them over. She stacked the empty basket back in the pile, nearly knocking over a display of knives on the counter.

"Wow," she said as she righted the display board. "No offense, but these are pricey knives."

"No more than you'd pay in the Wesley hardware store."

"People pay this much for a pocket knife?"

"They do if it's a Case. Rancher's favorite. Handles are real bone."

"I see."

"Nice Christmas gift," Anne said. "You know, maybe a souvenir for someone back home."

Madeline laughed. "I don't think my grandmother has much use for a pocket knife." But Connor might...no. Connor was not a knife guy. He was more of a safety-scissors man. "Thanks, anyway."

The post office was closed, so Madeline's last stop

before driving back to the ranch was the empty school parking lot. When she opened the phone, she was surprised to find a voice-mail indicator and four text messages. She hadn't even checked her phone until now. Amazing how she'd managed to wean herself off something that had been so essential just weeks before. And the strange thing was that she hadn't missed her phone after the first few days. Staying out of contact was surprisingly freeing.

She opened the first text message from Connor. Call me. The second. Call me now. The third. Are you getting these messages? Call me!

Madeline's heart was hammering by the time she hit the fourth message. Had something happened to her grandmother?

The fourth message calmed her slightly. Eileen is fine. Call me.

The voice mail was from Everett, who wanted to pass on some breaking news from the rumor mill before she heard it elsewhere—meaning Connor, no doubt. Madeline's mouth went dry as she listened. She tried to swallow, but couldn't get her throat muscles to work. His final words were, "Don't worry. I'll handle this. I repeat, don't worry."

She pushed the button to end the voice-mail message and sat staring up the snowy mountain road and thinking how glad she was that she wasn't in New York. Because if she was, she might just kill Dr. Jensen, her *mentor,* who had just publicly come out and hung the blame for using the blood on her, saying that she'd physically taken the samples from the lab, and lied to him about procuring permission. That she'd set him up, and his only crime was not double-checking his trusted assistant's claims.

Connor had been right. Jensen was a snake.

Her fingers shook as she punched in Everett's office number. After the phone clicked into the official welcoming message, she realized it was Sunday. Either Everett wasn't at the office or he was pretending not to be there so he could work in peace.

She left a short message at the voice-mail prompt: "Call me immediately if you find out anything else." She would have left Ty's number if she had it. But she could call for messages from his phone. Heck, she could call Everett from his phone.

It wasn't until a ranch truck drove by and slowed as if the driver was ascertaining whether she needed help that she snapped out of her funk. She waved at him, then started her car and put it in gear. She stopped again, long enough to fire a text message off to Connor saying that she knew about Jensen, and she'd talk to him soon.

When she got home, she set her bag of unnecessary groceries on the counter and dropped her coat and scarf on the sofa bed.

It's not that bad. Everett will handle it. It's not that bad.

But it felt that bad. She hated feeling helpless. Hated the powerlessness of her position. Hated Dr. Jensen. What a jerk.

She wanted to hole up and lick her wounds for a few

weeks. She also wanted to catch the next flight to New York and make a few public announcements herself.

Everett would kill her.

So she paced.

Every now and then she'd stop for a few minutes, then leap to her feet and pace again. Then, for want of anything better to do, she went to see Sling Cow.

"How's it going, girl?"

Sling Cow blinked and went back to chewing her cud.

"Ty says you seem to be getting some feeling back. Won't it be nice to be back out in the cold field with the other cows? Or are you faking it so you can be here, in the nice warm barn? I know what I would do in your position. Nice warm barn."

Madeline rested her forearms on the cool metal of the rails, then settled her chin on top, watching the cow watch her.

"I've been blindsided, girl. A wallop out of the blue. From someone I trusted." She put her forehead where her chin had just rested, squeezing her eyes shut. "Shit."

More west-of-the-Mississippi cursing, but the word felt utterly satisfying. Maybe she should shout it a few times. She looked back up at the cow. "It stinks when you trust someone, think you know someone and then... *pow!* It absolutely stinks."

MADELINE WAS TALKING to herself.

No. She was talking to the cow.

Ty wasn't certain which was worse. Yes, he talked to animals, but she was pouring out her guts.

"You okay?" he called, keeping his distance so she wouldn't think he was eavesdropping.

She whirled around, her cheeks growing pink.

"It's okay," he said, walking toward her, although he had a feeling she would rather have him disappear at that moment. "I wasn't listening. I just heard your voice." He smiled slightly, trying to reassure her. "I figured it had to be you, and if it wasn't, then I had myself a late-night television act." He pointed at the animal. "Talking cow," he explained, when she continued to stare at him.

"Yeah. I get it." She moistened her lips. "I was working some stuff out, and it helps me keep it clear if I say it out loud."

"So you weren't talking to the cow."

She opened her mouth to respond, then closed it again. He'd never seen Madeline so uncertain, so... vulnerable before. And it concerned him.

"Bad joke," he said by way of an apology.

"Not a joke," she responded. "I was talking to the cow."

"About anything in particular?" He moved a couple steps closer, trying to read her. He had the feeling that something unexpected had happened. She'd gone to town, then...

"Is your grandmother all right?"

"Yes. She's fine." Madeline glanced down, speaking to the straw at her feet. "It's me that isn't doing so well." She looked up at him then, and again he was struck by the open vulnerability in her face. "My mentor fed me to the wolves."

A surge of protectiveness welled up inside of Ty. "How so?"

"I have this via the college rumor mill… Jensen has alleged that I stole the samples and lied to him about having permission. If that's true, then he's only guilty of academic negligence. Not double-checking permission."

"This rumor mill…it's pretty accurate?"

"Stunningly so."

He reached out to tuck some strands of hair behind her ear, her cheek soft beneath the tips of his fingers. Then he gently tilted her chin up and laid his open palm on her cheek, trying as best he could to offer a little comfort. He knew what it felt like to battle demons alone. "I'm sorry this happened to you."

"I can deal with it." Emotions he couldn't fully read fought it out in her green eyes. "It's just been one hell of a shock."

She leaned her cheek into his palm as she spoke, as if gaining strength from him. He didn't think she was even aware of what she was doing. He bent his head and lightly kissed her lips, just as she'd kissed his jaw the night before. She stilled, but didn't move away. For a second they stood toe-to-toe, his hand still cupping her cheek, then she rose up on tiptoe to meet his lips again. This time her mouth opened and she kissed him more deeply.

Ty didn't pull her close, didn't let the kiss go hard

and deep, as the more insistent and reactive parts of his anatomy demanded. But it wasn't easy. In fact it was a battle he was on the verge of losing when Madeline broke the kiss, drawing in a shaky breath as she lowered her heels back to the ground.

"Okay," she said.

"Okay," Ty echoed. After a moment of silence, he added, "I'm not going to say that was a mistake." Because if he did, Madeline would probably argue with him.

"No. It wasn't," she agreed, as she pushed the loose hair back from her forehead.

He thrust his hands into his pockets, so he couldn't do what he wanted to do.

"It'd probably be best, though—"

"I think we both have a handle on the realities of our situation," Madeline said, cutting him off. "Just...don't back off, okay, Ty? We can just be friends, but...don't back off."

He pulled in a breath as uneven as hers had been. "I'll try." It was the best he could do right now.

Ty WENT BACK INTO his house and spent a long moment studying the small Western bronze his mother had sent him. She'd written "Not a Christmas gift" in bold black letters on the cardboard, then below it had added in smaller letters, "and even if it is, you'd better damned well accept it because I love you. Mom."

So Ty had opened the box and pulled out a bronze of a cowgirl sitting with her dog, gazing off into the distance. Kind of sappy, even for his mother, but she'd sent it because the artist was a childhood friend who was making a name for himself in the Western art world, and the subject of the bronze was Ty's high-school girlfriend, Lacy. He'd almost married her, but they'd been young, and when they went to separate colleges, they'd grown apart. He'd loved her, though.

Bronze Lacy looked a little like Madeline.

Ty put the figure on top of the bookshelf, where he couldn't see it.

CHAPTER SEVENTEEN

FRIENDS. JUST FRIENDS.

Madeline kept repeating the word as she drove to town. That was what she'd promised him. She needed to abide by Ty's wishes and not maneuver him into her bed. Not easy when she kept noticing how well his jeans fit, and how ridiculously good he smelled when they dragged those hay bales in unison…and how awful it felt to occasionally see deep hurt in his eyes.

Focus, Madeline told herself as her tire caught an icy rut. It was Monday and Everett would be in the office. She needed to make it to a cell-phone service area so she could call him.

She phoned Connor first, however, parking in her usual spot on the edge of town near the elementary school.

"I was about to call Everett. Have you heard anything else?"

"It's quiet now that grades are in and the students are gone. Most of the staff are on vacation. Only the academic grunts, such as myself, will be around the next two weeks."

"That's right. Friday was the last day of classes." Madeline had never before missed that day, or the celebratory drinks with her colleagues. The department Christmas party.

She'd never before been guilty until proven innocent, either, but that was the position Dr. Jensen had put her in.

"I have to call Everett, Connor. I'll be in touch. Hug Grandma for me."

"Will do," he said with a laugh. Eileen did not appreciate hugs and let it be known. Madeline hung up and then pushed Everett's number with her thumb. The receptionist put her through.

"You got my message," Everett said instead of hello.

"I did."

"I figured Connor would tell you as soon as he could, and I didn't want you to worry."

"Why would I worry?" Madeline asked drily. "I mean, Jensen only announced that I was the perpetrator."

"More like leaked. And I don't think it was Jensen."

"Why?" Madeline demanded.

"I don't like to talk about evidence over the phone, Madeline. Just trust me that this will work in your favor. They made an error—which is why I don't think Jensen was involved in this ploy."

"If you won't talk about evidence over the phone, then I'm going to be in your office first thing tomorrow morning."

"Not during the holiday season. You'll never get a flight."

"Everett. Please. How confidential can it be?"

"It's not so much confidential as…" His voice trailed off momentarily and then he sighed. "We've discovered when the samples were taken though the lab logs. We also know when Jensen tested his samples. There's only one window of opportunity, and you, my dear, were away from your job for two weeks during that time."

Madeline put a hand to her head. "You mean…"

"When your brother passed away," he said gently. "You were in Maine, making the funeral arrangements."

She closed her eyes. She hadn't left Eileen alone once during that time.

"Madeline?"

"I'm here." And she was still grappling with the fact that she had a clear alibi. Someone had tried to stick it to her and had accidentally stuck himself.

"This will shorten the process, but I'm afraid we'll have to go through both inquiry committee and the investigative committee. They aren't going to simply take my word on this."

"I understand." She didn't like it, but she understood.

"How are things on the ranch?"

"You wouldn't believe me if I told you."

"Maybe we can have dinner when you come back. I'll fill you in on the case and you can tell me about the ranch."

"Thanks, Everett. I owe you."

"Indeed you do," he said with a laugh. "But I'll pay for dinner."

Madeline fought a smile. She could go home. She could return to the campus, go back to her job without embarrassment. Go back to her old life.

In an odd way she was going to miss the ranch. Parts of it, anyway.

Madeline tucked her phone into her pocket and started the car, but instead of turning around and heading back up the mountain, she drove on to the mercantile. The jingle bells rang as she opened the door, and Anne looked up from her solitaire game.

"Will you take a debit card?" Madeline asked.

"Is it stolen?"

"Is that a prerequisite?"

Anne cackled. "Good one. I take plastic. Short on cash?"

"Getting there. I'll take one of these rancher knives."

"Outfitting yourself?" Anne asked as she removed one from the display.

"Arming my lawyer," Madeline replied. He deserved a souvenir of the Wild West. She thought for a moment, then said, "Make that two knives."

Anne smiled. "You're becoming my favorite customer."

"I can't arm my lawyer without arming my business partner."

"Getting Ty a knife, eh?"

"He's earned it," Madeline said. "I'm not the easiest person to deal with."

"You are different from your brother," Anne agreed.

"I have boxes for these in the back. Give me a minute and I'll get them." She came out from behind the counter. "I wrap for three bucks more."

"In that case, I'd like them wrapped."

TY WOULD BE GLAD when Madeline flew back to New York and he didn't have to worry every time she took to the road.

Or so he told himself when she drove in through the gate. He'd probably still think about her, but she wouldn't be so close.

He walked past the silversmithing shed without looking at it. He still wasn't ready to go inside.

She holed up in her house for the remainder of the day. He could see her through the window, working on her book, when he walked by. She must not have gotten any more bad news, or if she had she was keeping it to herself. He'd just finished washing his few dishes that evening when she knocked on the door.

"Hi," she said when he stepped back so she could come inside.

"No troubles on your trip to town?"

"I made it."

"I can see that," he said as he closed the door. "Any news on the professional front?"

"I think it's all going to work out. My lawyer found new information and I have an alibi."

"Airtight?" he asked, thinking she should be happier at the news.

"Skip's funeral."

Ty felt his barriers start to rise, but fought the reaction as best he could. He couldn't shut down now. Madeline might need to talk.

She studied his face for a moment, obviously trying to read him, before she said, "I'm going to be leaving in five days, and, well, here." She pulled a box out of her pocket. "Something for you to remember me by when you feed."

Ty knew what it was. He'd received knives as gifts before, from his father and his grandfather. He also remembered the very nice display of Case knives Anne put up every Christmas.

"I can't accept this."

"Why?"

"I appreciate the thought, Madeline, but…I can't."

"Don't you mean won't?" Her chin jerked up, but she couldn't hide the hurt in her eyes.

He should have taken the knife and put it with the bronze. But if he'd done that he would have been perpetuating a situation he didn't think would be good for either of them in the long run.

"We barely know each other," he finally muttered. Even if he *wanted* to know her better now that he'd scratched the uptight surface and found the tractor-racing woman below.

"Do you honestly believe we're nothing more than acquaintances?"

He couldn't bring himself to say yes.

Point to her.

"I can't let it be more," he said roughly.

"I just want to be your friend, Ty. Why can't we do that?"

"Why are you making me spell it out?"

"Because it's eating away at you."

"Damn it, Madeline."

"I loved my brother," she interjected hotly. "I think about him every day. I miss him. But I have learned to live without him, to accept what happened, even if I hate it."

"But you didn't kill him."

His words didn't have the effect he'd expected. If anything, Madeline looked angrier.

"Quit doing this." She reached up and grabbed him by the front of his shirt, twisting the fabric in her fingers, stopping just short of shaking him. "Get some help, Ty."

He took her wrists and pulled her hands away from his shirt. They dropped limply to her sides and she stared at him, her expression unreadable. He picked up the wrapped box from the counter and pressed it into her grasp.

"I've taken enough from you already. I'm not taking gifts on top of it."

Madeline dropped the box back onto the counter, where it landed with a thunk. "No. You're making excuses so you can keep flagellating yourself. Have fun, Ty."

MADELINE MARCHED BACK to her house through the darkness, wiping the back of her bare hand under her eyes, smearing angry tears across her cheeks, which in turn froze and burned. What was wrong with her? Why did it matter this much? And how was it that this guy could make her lose control? She prided herself on being calm and collected, even in a crisis such as losing her job.

Okay, maybe she made the occasional instant decision, but she didn't just snap, as she'd just snapped back there.

Why did his pain feel so much like her own?

Because she knew this pain too well. Knew that facing it head-on was the only remedy. It never went away, but the sharpness dulled to a level you could deal with. But Ty liked his pain sharp. He was honing it, keeping it at the cutting edge.

She couldn't help him, couldn't force him to get help if he didn't want to change.

No more. It hurt too much arguing with him.

TY THOUGHT THAT once Madeline left, once she accepted the inevitable, the worst would be over. Once again he was stunned by his own stupidity.

The worst wasn't over. He had to tell her the whole truth. Then it would be over. He went to the peg next to the door and got his coat. Alvin sprang to his feet, ready to go tackle whatever job was at hand.

"You stay here," Ty said. The collie's ears drooped. "Trust me on this one," he added, then let himself out the door.

"Madeline," he called as he stepped out onto the

path between their places. She was halfway to her dark trailer.

"What?" she yelled back, turning and putting her hands on her hips.

"I'm sorry."

"You're certainly right about that." She stomped on through the snow. Ty caught up with her in spite of the stiff knee. He took hold of her arm, stopping her.

"Madeline…this is complicated."

"No kidding. Now leave me alone. You achieved your objective. I'm backing off and you can continue to wallow in your misery. Status quo is the name of the game."

"Shut up, Maddie. I don't *want* to wallow in misery."

"What in the hell *do* you want?"

"I want my old life back," he said roughly.

Fat snowflakes started drifting down, melting as they hit her face. Madeline wiped the dampness off her cheek. "You can't have that. You have to start a new life. Deal with the accident."

"It wasn't an accident."

Madeline drew back. "What do you mean?"

"Skip didn't want to keep driving that night. He wanted to stop, but I insisted. I wanted to get to my mom's place instead of wasting fifty bucks on a motel. Fifty bucks. It was one of the only arguments we'd ever had. Skip was pissed, but gave in." Ty stared past her at the darkened window, seeing his grim reflection looking back at him.

"He made a decision. You didn't tie him up and force him."

His eyes snapped back to her face. Her simple statement, spoken in such a cool, accepting way, made him want to throw something. "How can you be that cold?"

"I'm not cold, Ty. I'm realistic." She put up a hand. "I grieved. I grieved for a lost brother, a lost future. I grieved for the unfairness. I cried buckets."

Ty drew in a breath. "So why don't you hate me?"

"I did," she said. "I hated you for months. But I bowed to reality, Ty. Long before we met. You wouldn't have driven on had you known what was ahead. You weren't drunk. You weren't reckless. You wanted to get home for Christmas."

He felt as if she hit him. He opened his mouth to ask how she knew what he'd never confessed to another soul, when she said calmly, "Skip called me when you stopped for gas that night. Told me you guys would be at your mother's house before morning."

Madeline waited for him to say something. What? What the hell could he say? He didn't even know what to think right now.

The snow was melting into her hair, dampening it, making it start to curl. And then, when he was about to go back to his house, to a nightmare, no doubt, she said softly, "Have you ever heard of forgiveness, Ty?"

He couldn't bring himself to answer. He turned and started walking, leaving Madeline alone in the snow.

CHAPTER EIGHTEEN

THE NEXT MORNING WAS appropriately gray and dreary. Madeline was still in bed, one arm draped over her eyes to combat the pressure of the headache she'd woken up with, when she heard the tractor start. Ty out on his lonely mission to care for the stock.

He wanted to be alone. Alone was what he did best. That way he could stay in his own painful world.

You can't help someone who isn't ready to help himself.

But that didn't mean you couldn't hurt for them. He was cracking open old wounds that she'd already healed. Making her hurt again.

Making her relive the pain herself, talk herself through it.

If he hadn't driven on instead of getting a room, then Skip might still be alive. But she didn't know how he could have controlled having cows in the road on the far side of a curve. That could have happened at any time.

The tractor revved once or twice, then he put it in gear, the noise growing louder as he left the barn.

She could still see him walking away last night. Choosing guilt over forgiveness.

Madeline rolled over, pressing her forehead against the cool leather of the sofa, pulling the sleeping bag up a little higher. Ty would turn the power on when he got back. She closed her eyes, felt the moisture of unshed tears—for her or for him?—and tried to ease her headache by going back to sleep.

TY ENDURED THE DAY from hell, followed by the night from hell. Madeline stayed holed up in her house, probably writing her book. A few more days and she'd be gone, and it appeared as if she'd be hiding out until then.

Since confessing to her, and finding out she'd known the circumstances all along…he was still dealing with that bombshell…he'd been unable to fall back into the old routine. His tried-and-true survival techniques didn't seem to be working, perhaps because what he was experiencing didn't feel so much like guilt as fear. But he wasn't sure what that fear was.

Fear of facing the truth, maybe?

He'd faced the truth so often he felt as if it was engraved in his flesh. He'd made a mistake and killed his friend.

Made a mistake.

Ty believed in forgiveness—in theory, anyway—even if he hadn't experienced a lot of it. His mother had never forgiven his father for leaving her, or herself for not holding on to him. His father had never forgiven himself for losing the last of the once vast family acreage down in the valley—the place where Ty used to visit every summer. His family were hard on themselves, hard on one another.

He needed to be hard on himself. It was the only way he could face each day. Freaking survivor's guilt.

Ty paused. He'd never given it a name before.

THE NEXT MORNING the cow was struggling in the sling.

Okay. One small miracle. He built a panel fence around the animal, then released her. She was wobbly, but could use her hindquarters. Disaster had been averted and a valuable animal saved.

He'd give her several days to regain her strength before he turned her back out with the others. Not that she'd minded being alone in the protection of the barn over the past two weeks. He'd reflected more than once on how unusual it was for a cow not to miss the herd. But hell, he didn't miss other people.

Liar. He felt he didn't deserve people in his life.

Ty walked out the wide equipment door, sliding one half-closed and then the other. And then he stood facing the padlocked shed.

He waded through the snow to the door and lifted the lock with one finger. The key was in his house.

MADELINE HAD JUST finished straightening her hair when Ty knocked on her door. She considered ignoring him, but after the past two days of voluntary mutual avoidance...well, he probably wouldn't be knocking unless it was important.

Ty stood for a moment on the snowy steps before entering the trailer. He carried something in one hand, but Madeline couldn't see what it was until she closed the door. He held out two pieces of curved metal.

"I don't know if you want them, but these are the spurs Skip was working on before he died."

Madeline's mouth opened, but she couldn't find words. "I put the rowels on them this morning. Other than that, it's all Skip. He cut the metal, forged the spurs and put the silver on one of them. The other one...didn't quite get finished."

"Did he do the engraving?" Madeline asked, taking the spur with the silver, her fingers brushing against the cool skin of Ty's hand. She ran her thumb over the polished surface of the spur.

"Yeah," Ty said. "He showed promise. Most beginners don't get cuts that deep using hand tools." He swallowed and glanced away.

Madeline reached out for the other spur, the plain one with no silver attached. "What part is the rowel?"

"The thing that spins on the end."

She nodded, pressing her lips together. The spurs were heavy, the metal smooth. And she was so damned torn and uncertain about...everything. She looked up at Ty at the exact same moment he brought his eyes back to her. This time she swallowed and then, less than a second later, her arms were wound around his neck and she was pressing her face into the warm hollow of his shoulder. His arms closed around her tightly. Almost too tightly, but Madeline didn't care.

"I want them," she said against his warm skin. "The spurs." She raised her head so she could see his face. "Thank you."

He cleared his throat. "No problem."

"I don't think that's true," she said.

"Madeline..." He gently brushed the hair away from her face. "I've got stuff to work through. We both know that."

For a moment they stared at each other and then Madeline said, "I'm leaving in a couple days."

"I know."

She teetered for a moment at the edge of the precipice, then took the leap. "Can you stay here with me? For a while?"

She could see that he understood her meaning perfectly. "What would that solve?"

"I think we should find out," she said, a little surprised at the husky note in her voice. "I think it will help both of us."

He moved closer, still not touching her. "Both of us."

"Yes." He was so close that she barely had to move to kiss the underside of his jaw, where she'd kissed him before, in the doorway. "Please?"

Ty pushed her hair back over her shoulders, then took her face in his hands and kissed her in turn, gently at first. But the heat grew so rapidly that Madeline wasn't quite sure how she ended up with her back against the door.

She loved kissing Ty Hopewell, and she wanted to do a sight more than kissing.

When she pushed his jacket over his shoulders, he let it fall to the floor. When she took off his hat, surprised at the weight of the heavy felt, he didn't protest. And when she started undoing buttons, half afraid that he was going to stop her, he instead returned the favor.

Madeline bit her lip as his rough fingers undid the first button on her white blouse, and then another, feeling the heat build inside her.

She pushed her hands up through his crisp dark hair, pulling his lips down to her level and kissing him, hoping against hope that he wouldn't let himself think too much, wouldn't withdraw. She had no doubts about what she was doing. She needed to help this man she'd come to care about. Help him back to the land of the living.

Ty didn't say a word as he undressed her, but she could see that he liked what he saw. The feeling was more than mutual. His stomach was incredible, his thighs lean and strong. When she knelt to peel his boxers down and let his erection spring free, she couldn't help running her tongue around the end of it. Ty looked both shocked and pleased at her boldness, but he pulled her back up to her feet before swinging her up into his arms and carrying her the rest of the way to her sofa bed.

It wasn't difficult to deduce that Ty hadn't been with a woman in a while and that he wanted the full Monty rather than a quick release.

He laid her down, then stretched out beside her,

running his hands over her almost reverently, kissing her. Exploring. Madeline did the same. She'd never touched such a solidly muscled man before, couldn't seem to get enough of him. But Ty needed more and so did she. When he rolled her onto her back she wrapped her legs around him, welcoming him without words.

His body shook as he entered her, from restraint or reaction, she didn't know, didn't care. Both were good, as long as he didn't overdo the restraint. The only reality was him filling her, pushing slowly into her, deeper and deeper. She gasped against his shoulder and then he kissed her, tenderly, before he started to move.

It had been months since she'd been with anyone, but she didn't think that was the reason she came before she was ready, bucking uncontrollably against him. Her entire body throbbed; her lips felt numb. She'd never reacted like this in her life and she really, really wanted to react like this again.

Ty's rhythm increased after she came, and he plunged into her almost desperately, as if this was his one and only shot at making love to her. If that was his intention, then Madeline was going to have to explain to him that he would have to change plans.

Just as she was building up again, he let out a low groan and poured himself into her. Madeline took his face between her hands and gently kissed his lips. His eyes were closed and sweat beaded his brow. He was gorgeous.

"I hope you're on the pill," he said, "and if you're not, then—"

"I'm on contraceptives."

He nodded against her shoulder and then collapsed on the mattress next to her, still half covering her, his penis still half hard inside her.

She loved the feeling of still being joined with him, didn't want it to end, but of course it did. Way too soon. After he slipped free, he put a heavy arm over her and shifted her body so her butt was pressed up against his groin. Then he pulled her even more tightly against him and promptly fell asleep.

WHEN TY WOKE he was hungry and horny. Two of his favorite feelings—when he had the means to do something about them.

Madeline made him feel alive again. Knowing that Skip had called her that night, that she'd been aware of the circumstances and had been able to forgive him... It humbled him.

She stirred against him and he moved his hand down to run a single finger over the junction of her thighs. She sighed.

"Mmm," she protested sleepily, although her legs moved apart, allowing his finger access to her slick center.

"Maddie," he whispered against her ear.

"I don't let people call me that," she murmured, her body tensing as his finger slipped inside. She let out a tiny moan, then drew air into her lungs from between her teeth. It seemed that she was now fully awake.

"Can *I* call you Maddie?"

She sucked in another sharp breath, her body jerking as he stroked her clit.

"Please?" he whispered.

"Ty…" She moved against his hand. "I don't…like nicknames.… Oh. My."

"Oh, my," he echoed, smiling against her shoulder, withdrawing his hand far enough to slide another finger in. Madeline gasped and tried to turn to face him, but he gently held her where she was. "Don't move, Maddie."

But she was moving. Against his fingers. He continued to stroke, glad he could give her pleasure, loving the feel of her butt grinding against his erection. Much more of this and he'd come before she did.

He was wrong. She came first, her entire body arching back against his before she gave in to a shuddering release.

This time when she tried to turn, he didn't stop her. Instead he smiled into her beautiful eyes and ruffled the silky curls on either side of her face. "Let me call you Maddie, let your hair go natural."

She drew back, shocked.

"No."

"Why?"

"No one takes a short person with curly hair seriously."

"I will."

She didn't look convinced. He grasped her waist and gently lifted her, and she reached down to guide him as he slowly impaled her. Ty smiled and then groaned as she started to ride him. Seconds later he didn't care what she let him call her or how she wore her hair.

Ty managed, for the first time in two years, to let himself exist in the here and now.

TY DID LITTLE BUT SPEND time with Madeline over the next three days. They moved hay, and he set mousetraps in the grain shed so she wasn't afraid to go inside. He took her into the workshop and showed her the silver-working tools.

Yeah, he still felt guilty, but it was falling into perspective. It was only a fluke that he was alive, but what right did he have to throw away the gift he'd been given? As Madeline had pointed out, it didn't make Skip any more alive.

But deep down, Ty knew it wasn't logic or arguments that helped him get a tenuous grip on his grief and guilt. It was Maddie's ability to love him in spite of what had happened. If she could forgive him, how could he not at least try to forgive himself?

Their lovemaking increased in intensity, and oddly, as it did, Madeline seemed to pull away. Nothing blatant, just a feeling he got. As if she needed a certain distance. And here he'd thought that was his role.

It was on their third night of sharing a bed—Madeline's sofa bed—that Ty broached the subject of the ranch.

"I'm not going to put it on the market," she said. "I can't do that to you."

Again, there was a distance between them. Maybe

she was thinking about leaving. He knew he was thinking about her leaving, about the emptiness. Funny, but living alone, being alone, had seemed so necessary up until Madeline.

"I want you to do it because being partners with me is beneficial to you," Ty said. He'd thought all evidence pointed to them making a rather decent team now that they understood each other.

"I'm sure it will be." Madeline shifted and pulled the covers up to her shoulders. More distance.

"How are we going to handle this?" he asked point-blank. He'd thought about it, but figured the subject would come up before she flew back home.

"I guess if you make a profit, you'll send me a check."

"Us."

Madeline's expression shifted and, being a master at barriers, he recognized the instant hers went up. "Not to be obtuse, but there's not much to handle. I'm going home. You're running the ranch."

"And we never make love again?"

"Ty...this is what it is. Two people making love because they care for one another. I value your friendship and if—when—we get together again, yes, we'll probably make love. It isn't like we don't have chemistry."

"You value my friendship?"

She reached over to touch his face. "You know I do."

He pulled back. "We're friends."

Her expression grew shuttered. "Yes."

"Bullshit. Friends don't make love like we do."

"They do if they're friends with benefits," she muttered, not meeting his eyes.

"You're delusional, Maddie. We are not just friends."

"We can't be anything else," she said stubbornly, looking up at him. He was stunned at the conviction in her voice. He got out of bed and stood naked in the cold, staring down at her. "And there's nothing wrong with a deep abiding friendship!" she added.

"Why can't we be anything else?"

Madeline sat up, the sheet pooling around her waist, her nipples hardening in the cold air. "Reality, Ty."

She'd shoved him, kicking and fighting, into facing the fact that he had a problem, and now that he was dealing with reality, she was generating a new reality?

"Care to expand on that answer, Professor?" he asked sardonically.

Her chin lifted. "Would you move to the East Coast? New York, to be exact?"

He stared at her as if she was crazy. "How would I earn a living there?"

"Exactly. And how would I earn a living here?"

"So you did this to snap me out of depression?" He was getting pissed. Talk about living in fantasyland during the past few days.

"I did it because I care for you, Ty. I'm glad we connected and I want to stay in contact, but...my place is back in New York and yours is at the ranch. All we can do is enjoy the here and now. Learn from it. Be friends." She held his gaze as she said softly, "I thought you understood."

"Screw being friends. I'm falling in love with you, Maddie."

"Don't say that."

"Why the hell not?"

"I'm not ready to hear it. And I don't know if you're ready to say it."

Okay, maybe they hadn't been together that long. But he knew what he was feeling. He'd felt it before—just not this strongly.

"Don't mistake love with gratitude," she said in that academic tone.

He drilled her with a dark look. "I know what gratitude feels like and I know what friendship feels like. You, on the other hand, may have some brushing up to do."

He needed to get out of there before he said something he would later regret—something he wasn't "ready to say."

He grabbed his clothes off the floor, considered walking back home naked, then decided not to be any stupider than he'd already been.

Madeline didn't say a word as he dressed, or as he let himself out of the trailer. He slammed the door. It bounced open and he had to shut it again, before stalking off down the path to his house, which looked even lonelier than it had when he'd left it that morning.

What now?

His life had been one hell of a lot easier when he'd spent it going through the motions.

AFTER THE DOOR CLOSED, Madeline fell back onto the sheet and tried to hold in tears that for once didn't concern her brother. This was no longer about Skip. It was about Ty. And her.

Okay, she'd gotten her wish. Ty had eased up on himself. He was starting the journey to self-forgiveness.

But she hadn't wanted him to fall in love. They lived on opposite sides of the country, in practically opposite existences. Her life wouldn't transplant well to the ranch, and his to New York…? Even he'd had to admit that was out of the question. Not much call for his line of work back there.

So had she helped or hindered?

She pulled the sheet up under her chin and turned her head to the side as hot tears ran over her cheeks onto the pillow that still smelled like Ty.

What had she done?

And how could she undo it?

CHAPTER NINETEEN

WHEN TY GOT UP TO feed the next morning, there was a folded note tucked in his door, and Madeline's car was gone.

The note fluttered down to the snowy steps when he stepped out. He picked up the paper and shook it off.

Dear Ty—

"Dear, my ass," he muttered. He gritted his teeth and read on.

I'll be in contact about the ranch within the next few months. Until then, take care.
Yours,
Madeline

Ty set the paper on the counter, stared at it for a few minutes, then snatched his jacket off the hook and left the house, Alvin at his heels.

Stand-and-face-the-music, meet-reality-head-on Madeline was on the run. So who was the coward now?

At least she hadn't put anything about not wanting to hurt him into the letter. He was sure she didn't want to hurt him. He was equally certain that she'd failed in that regard.

He stopped short.

He wasn't done with this situation between them. Not by a long shot.

Ty turned on his heel and started back toward the house, much to Alvin's obvious confusion. The dog kept bumping Ty's leg with his nose, as if to remind him that he was going in the wrong direction.

"I know, bud. We'll start in a minute."

Madeline's scheduled flight didn't leave until the next day, but there was always standby. Was she waiting in the airport right now for a plane?

No, she couldn't have gotten to the airport yet, unless she'd left just after he'd stalked back to the house. He hadn't fallen asleep until after 3:00 a.m., so she had to be on the road.

It was close to Christmas, too, and flights had to be packed. So what was her plan?

He tried to think like Madeline, but he wasn't that confident in his abilities.

She would take her scheduled flight back home. All she was doing was leaving early and avoiding another scene with him. Hell, for all he knew, he'd hurt her feelings, too.

The sane thing would be to wait the few months until she felt like contacting him. Much to Alvin's relief, Ty turned back around and headed to the barn, glad he didn't have any neighbors to watch him walk in circles.

He pulled open the barn doors and started the tractor, determined to make this just another day. However, feeding didn't bring the peaceful satisfaction it usually did.

He was pissed.

Madeline had been good for him. The ranch had been good for her. When he thought about the uptight, brittle woman who'd showed up at the gate four weeks before and compared her to the woman he'd made love to, the woman who'd made love to him, well, friendship might be a wonderful bond, but they had more than that. Whether she wanted to admit it or not.

And she'd accused him of living in denial.

If she didn't want a relationship, then she didn't. He couldn't force her, and her points about where they lived were valid. But Maddie hadn't even tried to discuss the matter.

She hadn't said goodbye.

When he got back to the house he fed Alvin, then disconnected his cell phone from the charger. He dug through his important-papers drawer until he found the business card Madeline had given him a couple days ago, with both her grandmother's and her assistant's phone numbers on the back. Which one?

He'd go with the assistant. He entered the number, and a prim male voice answered.

"Is this Connor?" Ty had no idea what the kid's last name was.

"It is." Connor whatever-his-last-name-was sounded cautious.

"This is Ty Hopewell. Madeline's business partner in Nevada?" Ty spoke briskly, matter-of-factly, as if he had no plans to scam the poor guy. "She left for the airport early this morning and I just found something I think she's going to want. I've tried to call, but she's out of service range."

"Would you like the mailing address?"

"I'd like to know what time her flight takes off. I may be able to catch her." He was hoping she was holed up in Reno somewhere and he'd have some time to find her and get a few things off his chest before she jetted out of his life.

"What did she leave behind?" Connor asked warily.

"Her little computer," Ty said, hoping that a big lie was more believable that a small one.

"Madeline left her netbook?"

"It was at my place. I think she packed the case without looking inside. It's pretty small and light."

There was a lengthy pause. Ty swore he could hear his heart beating. "Yeah, I guess I can see that happening," the kid said.

"I'll be happy to mail it to her, though." Ty did a pretty good impression of offhandedness. That seemed to decide the matter.

"I think she'll want it, if you can get it to her. Her flight leaves at eight-thirty tomorrow morning. It's a Delta flight."

"Thanks."

Okay, that gave him a little time. He dialed Manny

Hernandez, the local do-anything guy, and asked if he could feed the next day. Manny agreed, as long as it could be at noon, since he was plowing in the morning.

"No problem," Ty said, although the cows might not be happy at breakfast being delayed. "I'll leave a check on the seat of the tractor."

He hung up and thought for a moment. He'd covered the ranch chores; he knew what time Maddie's flight left and what airline it was. Now all he needed to do was to find her.

Thank goodness Reno had a smallish airport.

It took Ty exactly half an hour to shower, pack and get into his truck, leaving a dejected Alvin pouting. The collie had plenty of food and a doggy door into the enclosed porch. He was going to have to handle the ranch alone for twenty-four hours.

Ty hadn't had closure with Skip. He was damned well going to get it with Madeline.

IT WASN'T DIFFICULT to find Madeline at the airport. He simply got there at dawn—feeding time—and waited at the top of the stairs leading to the security gate until she showed up. If anyone had a problem with him loitering there for well over an hour, they never said a word. Christmas carols played in the background, interrupted every now and then by the public service announcements regarding airport safety.

He'd tensed up during the first few songs, but as time went on, he found that he was concentrating so hard on not missing Maddie that the songs that had once given him flashbacks became background noise. He didn't come close to having to step outside and take a reality break. But Bing Crosby didn't sing, either. Ty was better, but he wasn't ready for Bing.

As he waited, he considered exactly what he wanted to accomplish with this meeting—better late than never, he figured, because up until now he'd been running on instinct. A public scene? Tears? Acrimony?

No. He wanted to end what they had with something more than a note tucked into the door. He might have had his jerk moments, but he deserved more than a note.

Finally, just before seven o'clock, he saw her. She was fighting suitcases, which were strapped to some ridiculous metal rolling frame, onto the escalator.

He waited until she'd pulled the contraption off the escalator before stepping forward and blocking her path.

"Hi, Maddie."

"Ty." One single word. *Ty.* Nothing else. No apology. No explanation. Just wide-eyed guilt.

"I got your note."

She wheeled her suitcases to the side, getting out of the path of the people trying to leave the escalator.

Her cheeks flushed pink. "I'm sorry for leaving the way I did."

"Yeah. I figured."

She inhaled deeply before facing off with him. "So what now, Ty?"

"I imagine you're going to get on that airplane and fly back home."

She frowned. "So you came all this way…"

"To say goodbye."

Her lips parted for a moment and her frown deepened.

"I never got to say goodbye to Skip," he continued in a low voice. "I wanted to say goodbye to you."

"Goodbye?" she asked warily.

"See? Wasn't that easy?" He leaned forward and planted a kiss on the smooth skin of her cheek. "Goodbye, Madeline."

He was halfway down the escalator when Bing started to croon, "It came upon a midnight clear…"

Ty barely noticed.

MADELINE WAITED UNTIL she hefted her bag off the other side of the security X-ray belt before glancing over her shoulder. Ty was really gone.

Coming after her to say goodbye was quite an effective way of showing exactly how insensitive she'd been, taking off in the early hours of the morning without a word. She'd convinced herself that it was the best thing to do—easier on both of them, since she'd so obviously kicked him in the teeth the night before.

She was wrong. It had been cowardly, and she was ashamed of both her behavior and her attempt to justify it to herself. But regardless of how poorly she'd handled the situation, their two worlds were not going to mesh. It would be more like worlds colliding. The matter was done; it had to be done, because there was no place for it to go.

So why the heck did it feel so much like unfinished business?

Madeline tried to fall asleep as soon as the plane took off, since she hadn't slept much the night before, but no luck. Her seatmate wanted to talk, about grandkids, weddings, her neighbors. Madeline endured politely until she changed planes in Chicago, but by that time she was too wired to sleep.

Connor met her at the airport ten minutes late, wearing pressed khaki pants and a Barbour overcoat, the blond cowlick at the back of his head sticking up as if he'd been running his hand over his hair. Late *and* dressed up?

"Christmas shopping," he explained. "I'm helping out some of Eileen's friends."

"That's sweet, Connor."

He nodded, looking blatantly uncomfortable, and she didn't think it had anything to do with Christmas shopping.

"What?" she prompted.

"Did you get your netbook?"

"My what?"

"I thought so."

"What?" Madeline asked again.

"I fell for that cowboy-rancher guy's ruse. He called to find out what flight you were on, and it was only later that I started to get suspicious."

Well, that explained how he knew what staircase to stake out.

"It's all right," Madeline said, patting Connor's arm as they went outside. The air was moister in New York. Moister and colder.

"But—" he began to protest.

"No, really. It's fine. He just wanted to say good-bye."

Rip her heart out and say goodbye.

MADELINE WAS SO GLAD to see her grandmother, to catch up on family news, to pretend she hadn't just done the most cowardly thing she could ever remember doing—leaving Ty the way she had. She was glad to slip back into a life where she was grounded and knew what to expect. Glad she had family.

They visited Skip's grave together on Christmas Eve, then went to services immediately after. That evening Connor joined them for the raucous Christmas party at the retirement community. Several of her cousins were there, and Madeline spent a lot of time as the center of attention, answering questions about the ranch, which, quite frankly, she didn't even want to think about. The experience had left her raw and off-kilter.

As she ducked a kiss under the mistletoe from her grandmother's inebriated friend, Mr. Carlton, a retired geophysicist, she thought about Ty. How was he spending Christmas? Alone, as he planned? The thought made her ache.

Hell, everything made her ache, and now she was

cursing on the east side of the Mississippi. In her head, anyway.

Yes, she'd known she would miss him, but not to this degree. Hurt as it might, she couldn't allow emotions to overcome logic. She'd spent years—decades really—building a stable, sensible existence that didn't transplant well. Not much call for an anthropology professor in the rural West. She had a home, family, a job…maybe… here. Everything she needed was here. Except for Ty. But that need would fade.

She couldn't imagine what her life would be like if it didn't.

"Are you sure you don't want to play?" Connor called from over at the kitchen table, where two of the cousins, plus a retired botanist and another anthropologist, were gearing up for a game of Risk.

"No, thank you," Madeline called, and Connor made an exaggeratedly perplexed face. She usually did enjoy conquering the world, but not tonight. She could barely handle her own life tonight.

So, while Connor's group was happily destroying each other's armies in the dining area, and everyone else was gathered near the food, noshing, Madeline sat on the sofa with Eileen. She sipped red wine that had no effect on her whatsoever, and filled in her grandmother about the operation of the ranch. It was a conversation she hadn't been looking forward to, and this seemed a good opportunity to get it over with—while there was a bottle of disappointingly ineffective wine nearby.

"I have the figures and the, uh, calendar to show you next time I come."

"Have you made a decision about selling?" Eileen asked when Madeline was done explaining the general operations.

"I have," she said. "For now I want to leave things the way they are." She owed Ty that much.

"So you trust Mr. Hopewell now?"

"Yes," she replied, staring into the propane fire. She couldn't find words to explain to her grandmother the complicated relationship between her and Ty. "I learned a lot at the ranch." The irony of the words made it hard to say them with a straight face. "Enough to know he's running a decent operation in a tough market."

"You seem distracted since returning. I thought perhaps your time at the ranch had been unpleasant."

Madeline pulled her gaze away from the bluish flames to meet her grandmother's gaze, and said sincerely, "It's the season, Grandma. And the upcoming hearings."

Nothing to do with being heartsick about how she'd led a decent guy on, only to dump him on his butt.

She gave her grandmother what she hoped was a reassuring smile. "Once I get the hearings over with, I'll be fine."

THE HEARING HAD BEEN postponed. Ten days. It was legal according to the university policy manual, and it was also a deliberate move by Dr. Mann in her capacity as department head, to make sure Madeline wouldn't be able to start spring classes. Madeline was certain of it, and she told Everett her theory when they met for lunch on the day the hearing had originally been scheduled for.

"I agree," he said matter-of-factly, sipping a glass of zinfandel. Madeline wondered idly what Amuma might do to him. Everett was always under control, and he was one of the few men Madeline knew who could make a receding hairline look sexy. Something about the easy confidence in his very blue eyes...even though she rather preferred dark eyes now. "But we'll get you reinstated."

"When?" she asked grimly. She pushed her quiche around her plate. Lunch was a bad idea, even if Everett was paying and not billing her for it. "I guess this is what happens when you tell the department head that her policies are shortchanging the students who are paying for an education.

"Bring in more funding to the department and you can say whatever you like." Everett, who had years of experience handling academic misconduct cases, had discussed this with her more than once. Besides being a thorn in Dr. Mann's side, Madeline didn't bring in funding. Her career was too new and she spent more time teaching than researching. Jensen brought tons of grant funding into the department, so of course Dr. Mann wanted Madeline to take the fall. After that, Dr. Jensen could be reprimanded for academic negligence—for not double-checking those pesky permissions—and everything would be fine in the anthropology department. Unless your name was Madeline Blaine.

"Eat, Madeline. You don't want to look gaunt and worried at the hearing."

"Fine. I'll eat," she said, scooping some of the side salad onto her fork. "But you know what?" She made a small circle with her fork after popping the lettuce in her mouth. "It isn't so much starting classes that bugs me…it's being played. I hate that they're doing this not in the name of finding out what really happened, but because they're trying to get things back to the status quo with as little impact to Dr. Jensen as possible."

"This is academia, Madeline. You know the game."

And maybe that was what she hated. The unspoken rules of the game. He who brought in funding was much more important than she who actually taught—which, unless Madeline was sadly mistaken, was one of the purposes of a college. To teach.

"I don't know that I want to keep playing by their rules."

Everett set his glass down on the table. "Who are you?" He smiled as he said it, but he did look slightly mystified.

"Okay. Maybe I don't want to keep playing by their rules."

The lawyer settled back in his chair, reaching once more for this glass as he studied her. "Now you sound more like yourself."

If only she felt like herself.

What was happening to her? Had she lost her focus? Her drive? The stuff that made her so uniquely her?

An hour later she unlocked the door to her apartment and went inside, where she flipped a switch and, ta-da! The lights came on.

No noise, no breakdowns, no fuel. So easy.

For almost a week after coming back from the ranch, she'd forgotten to turn on the lights when she entered a room. Progress.

She barely finished putting away the groceries when her phone rang. A Nevada number. Her heartbeat raced.

Oh, dear heavens. It was him.

"Ty. Hello." Her heart was thudding so hard it was difficult to say hello in a normal voice.

"Hi, Madeline." He paused ever so briefly, then said, "I'm calling because I want to make an offer on your half of the ranch."

Madeline nearly dropped the phone. "How…?" And then she realized "how" was really none of her business. If he'd gotten financing, then he had. She moistened her lips. "This is a surprise."

"No doubt," he said coolly. "I can email the offer for you to look over, then you can get back to me."

"All right," she said numbly. Impulsively, she added, "How've you been?"

The silence that followed her question was significant. Oh, yeah, she'd given up all rights to answers to personal questions when she'd walked out on him. But she stubbornly waited for a response.

"I've been fine."

"Alvin?"

"He's also fine."

"Sling Cow?"

"Back in the herd."

"That's good news," Madeline said, forcing a note of enthusiasm into her voice, trying to hear a hint of the old Ty.

"Yeah. Well, if you'd look over the offer, I'd appreciate it. I talked to Kira and she'll handle the legal aspects of title transfer, etcetera."

"Sounds like you've got the ball rolling."

"I have. I'll email you a pdf copy of the papers as soon as I hang up."

Madeline closed her eyes, unexpectedly disappointed by his businesslike manner. He hadn't even asked about the hearings. She had truly burned her bridges with Ty.

TY HUNG UP THE PHONE. Mission accomplished, and he hadn't given in to Maddie's awkward attempts at burying the hatchet. He knew what she was doing, trying to bring things back to a friendly level, and he'd probably been a jerk not to play along. But he didn't want a friendship with her just now. Didn't know if he could handle it, so he wasn't going to try.

He went to his kitchen window and stared out over his pastures, watched his cattle eat. The ranch had given him a reason for being for almost two years. Until Madeline.

So here he was. Working on forgiving himself and making some headway. He still had moments, but he made it through the holiday season without going into a black funk. He'd even gone to church on Christmas, figuring that was the easiest way to ease back into the community. After the services, he'd stopped at the bar for a drink and people had been…accepting. Not pushy or overly friendly. He'd come close to enjoying himself.

The phone rang in his pocket and he checked the number before picking it up. His dad. Ty had called both his parents on Christmas, and, surprisingly, his father had offered the financial assistance he hadn't been able to extend two years ago. It seemed that selling his wife's house in California had left Ty's dad with a healthy profit—and a deep need to invest in property to avoid taxes.

So now Ty had a way out of owing Madeline, of being tied to her through business and through Skip's legacy.

The place would be his alone. All Madeline had to do was agree. He saw no reason why she wouldn't.

He only wished the thought wasn't so damned depressing.

"THERE ARE SO MANY choices." Eileen studied the headphone display for a moment before picking up a pair of noise-canceling Bose. She'd finally agreed to try an iPod, primarily because Connor had bought her one for Christmas and now the search for Madeline's present— acceptable headphones—was on.

Eileen clamped the display model on over her short white bob and turned to Madeline with a cheeky smile. "What do you think?"

"You look like you're about to direct a passenger jet out to the runway for takeoff."

Eileen nodded with satisfaction and put the earphones back on the display. "I want those."

"All right." Madeline found the box and avoided wincing at the price. This was her grandmother, after all.

"Did the Bickmans chip in?" Eileen asked on the way to the checkout counter.

"No." Madeline cut a mystified sideways glance at her grandmother. Why would Eileen's next-door neighbors chip in for a belated Christmas gift?

"Well, they should, since their complaints are what got Connor all gung ho on the iPod."

"Ah. I'll send them a bill for their half," she stated.

Eileen laughed. "Do that."

Madeline made the purchase and carried the bag to the car. She and her grandmother drove back to the retirement complex in silence, but it wasn't a comfortable one. Eileen had something to say. The question was when would she say it?

"What are you going to do?" Eileen asked when they arrived at her door. She was wearing that shrewd look that told Madeline to tread very, very carefully.

"About the job or the ranch?" Madeline had told Eileen about the offer before they'd set out on their shopping trip.

"There isn't much you can do about the job. The hearing process progresses at its own maddening, snaillike pace."

"The ranch, then," Madeline said. "I don't know yet." She followed her grandmother into her apartment, furnished in modern Danish, a style both she and Skip had always secretly hated, although it did set off Eileen's eclectic array of artifacts rather nicely.

Eileen placed the bag with the headphones on the small island that separated the kitchen from the living room. "I think the wisest move, since you do have an offer, is to sell. Settle one issue so you can focus on the other."

"Are *you* sure you want to follow that course?" Madeline asked, remembering the tears in her grandmother's voice not all that long ago. And secretly she hoped Eileen would say no. Then she had a legitimate excuse to wait longer, hold on to that tie that was doing her no good.

"I believe I am."

"What changed, Grandma?"

Eileen's smile was bittersweet. "Skip used to send me letters describing how beautiful the land was, how ornery the cows could be, how quiet it was at night. He said he could see millions of stars every clear night because there were no artificial lights to interfere with their brightness. I didn't totally understand it, but the ranch made him a happy man, and it holds a special place in my heart because of it." Eileen pulled her shoulders back slightly. "But the ranch hasn't made you happy and I think the time has come to sell, while we have this opportunity. I'm sorry I stopped you before. I just… wasn't ready."

"It isn't the ranch that made me unhappy," Madeline said, before stopping to think. The words simply fell out of her mouth.

"You haven't been the same since you've come back."

"I feel different," she agreed.

"Why?"

Madeline didn't have an exact answer. Hurting Ty was part of it. Knowing he wasn't going to forgive her was another. And…maybe it was the doubts she felt with increasing frequency, doubts about the life that she'd been so satisfied with before. It wasn't that she didn't still want that life…it was more a question of whether that life wanted her.

Eileen put her hands on Madeline's shoulders and squeezed gently. "I truly believe that once you sort out this job situation, everything else will fall into perspective. During unsettling times, and heaven knows I've had a few of those, raising you and Skip—" she smiled "—issues become monstrous. We're making no money off the ranch. The ranch was Skip's dream, not ours. I think you should sell."

TEN DAYS LATER, TWO DAYS before classes were to begin, Madeline showed up at the administration building for the hearing, wearing a navy blue suit and white blouse— her ultraprofessional suit. She met Everett just outside the door minutes before the proceedings began. He'd hurried from across town, and it showed. She reached up and straightened his slightly crooked gray striped tie.

"Are you ready for this?" she asked, concerned that ever-cool Everett look frazzled.

"That's my line, and yes," he said, taking over straightening the tie and then smoothing a hand over his sandy hair. "The cab driver was slightly insane, but I'm here." He shifted his briefcase to his other hand. "Are *you* ready?"

She was more than ready. Ten days spent cooling her heels had taken their toll. She'd received the ranch offer from Kira, with apologies, on Tuesday instead of Monday, so Madeline had had to ignore it for only five days, not counting today. She would make a decision after the hearing, and she'd emailed Kira to tell her, getting a quick "thanks" in return. So now the hearing was about to begin and then she'd have to look over the ranch offer.

Madeline lifted her chin as they were ushered into the room. This first step with the inquiry committee was basically a formality—a meeting in which full information would be given about the allegations to allow Madeline to prepare a response and suggest witnesses. Everett already knew the general allegations and was working on the response, but official hoops had to be jumped through.

She and Everett took their seats. Madeline kept her hands in her lap, sitting straight as she met the very serious gazes of the inquiry committee, the department head and the dean. They looked like the judge's panel on *Top Chef,* which she and her grandmother had watched the night before. Bad sign when she was thinking irreverent thoughts rather than focusing on proving her innocence. She sat up even straighter.

The chairman of the committee introduced the proceedings and began reading the allegations, which boiled down to Madeline having taken blood samples during finals week two years ago, while the lab had been unmanned for several days, and having misinformed Dr. Jensen about procuring the necessary permissions.

After the chairman had finished reading the allegations, Everett put down his pen and folded his hands in front of him.

"A question, if I may?"

"Of course."

"According to the lab records, work schedules and prior and subsequent use of the blood samples, the only window of opportunity is the one outlined here?"

"Correct."

Everett made a note and Madeline continued to stare impassively at the committee. Dr. Mann sat at one end of the table, a slight smile playing on her lips because she didn't yet know that she'd screwed up. She'd taken the position six months after Skip's death and wasn't aware that Madeline hadn't been around during the critical time frame when the blood samples had been taken.

But Jensen should have known.

Had he forgotten? Or perhaps hoped against hope that

Madeline and her lawyer would develop sudden cases of stupidity?

Or had he finally done the right thing, even if it was in the wrong way?

A few minutes later Madeline and her lawyer were dismissed from the room. Not one thing had happened in the short hearing that couldn't just as easily happened ten days before. She was definitely being jerked around.

"I'd say you're home free," Everett said as he escorted her from the building onto the freshly scraped sidewalk.

"Why didn't Jensen say something about the time frame?"

"You know that saying about gift horses?"

"Yes, but I never understood it."

"Leave it, Madeline." There was a note of warning in Everett's voice. "At least until we get you fully exonerated."

"And then what?" Madeline asked, the question aimed more at herself than her lawyer.

"You go back to work."

"Where things will never be quite the same."

"Did you expect them to be?" He sounded surprised.

In truth, she'd never given life after the hearings a thought. "Up until now I thought that once it became obvious I was innocent, everything would go back to normal. But did you see the look on Dr. Mann's face? She's out for blood."

"I'd say that's a safe assumption." Everett put a hand on Madeline's shoulder. She felt rather dense for having had such supreme confidence in the process of justice.

"I don't think I've been thinking straight since this all started. Maybe not since Skip died."

"Understandable," Everett said.

"I've made some mistakes."

"As have we all."

Her eyes flashed up to his face. "Are you humoring me?"

"No. I'm agreeing. You've made some mistakes." He brushed snow off his lapel. "Now the trick is to not make any more mistakes—at least not for a while."

CHAPTER TWENTY

EVERETT WOULD UNDOUBTEDLY have considered Madeline's next move a mistake. She stood on the front porch of Dr. Jensen's tasteful brick home and rang the bell. Then rang again when there was no answer.

You're going to be arrested for disturbing the peace, she thought as she stabbed the bell with her finger yet again. Or maybe trespassing, because she wasn't going to stop until she saw Dr. Jensen face-to-face.

She was about to ring again when she finally heard movement in the house and a few seconds after Mrs. Jensen, wearing a long pale blue satin robe, opened the door. All expression left the woman's normally pleasant face when she saw Madeline, then she pursed her lips so tightly they went white.

"You aren't supposed to be here."

Madeline was taken aback by the woman's vehemence. "Good evening, Edith. I need to see Phillip."

Edith's mouth tightened again before she said, "I don't think under the circumstances—"

A hand settled on Edith's shoulder and Dr. Jensen stepped into view, wearing a red plaid robe. Obviously the Jensens went to bed early. It was only eight o'clock. Madeline wondered how Dr. Jensen slept.

"Come in," he said, easing his wife aside and opening the door wider.

"I don't want to come in," Madeline said. And she didn't—she just wanted a few quick answers and it wasn't so cold outside that she couldn't hear them on the porch. "What in the hell is going on?"

"You'd best come inside."

"Fine." Madeline walked two steps into the foyer, just far enough so that Dr. Jensen could close the door. That's when she noticed how exhausted her former mentor looked. Drained, in fact. He had deep circles under his gray eyes, and he'd lost weight. His face, which had been gaunt before, was positively skeletal beneath his unruly dark gray hair.

Tough.

"What's going on, Phillip?" she asked. "Why is Dr. Mann under the impression I took those samples when you know damn well I couldn't have?" She cocked her head, regarding him through narrowed eyes. "Have you suddenly gone noble? Is your conscience getting the better of you?"

Color rose in his pale cheeks. "I was told to keep my mouth shut. So—"

"He only has two years left until retirement," Edith interrupted, as if it was Madeline's fault her husband was embroiled in this situation. "And we need the health benefits."

Jensen touched his wife's arm and she looked away from Madeline. "I'm keeping my mouth shut," he said as if Edith hadn't spoken. "Not that she confides in me in the first place."

Madeline folded her arms over her chest. "You're letting her hang herself? Even though...?"

"It will affect me? Yes."

Madeline wished she could feel a measure of gratitude, but this felt too little, too late.

"He didn't know about the permissions," Edith interrupted again. "None of this should have happened."

"That's ridiculous," Madeline said automatically.

"I skirted the issue," Jensen said in a low voice. "I assumed that since the blood was available for the medical studies, I could use it, too. I hadn't realized the permissions were so narrow. They've never been questioned before. I was stunned when this happened. The lawsuit..." He moved his head as if trying to shake off a nasty memory.

That didn't excuse him for *keeping his mouth shut* at her expense.

"What happens after she finds out I have an alibi?"

"That's anyone's guess, but, Madeline, she will continue to try to remove you from the department."

"That's happy news," Madeline muttered. "Is that why you didn't step forward on my behalf?"

Dr. Jensen didn't reply. He didn't need to.

"What about you after she finds out she's wrong?" Madeline asked.

"No telling." He pushed his hands deep into his robe pockets. "I may lose my job. I may not."

But regardless, unless Mann found a scapegoat, Dr.

Jensen's usefulness as a funding magnet would be over and that wouldn't bode well for his future.

He put his hand on his wife's shoulder and she covered it with her own, still not looking at Madeline. "I've never approved of what Dr. Mann is trying to do," he said.

"But you never did anything about it."

"No," he said softly. "I didn't. We need those health benefits for a few more years... I need my retirement."

MADELINE DIDN'T SLEEP that night. After leaving the Jensens, she honestly believed Dr. Jensen had assumed no one would question his use of the blood samples. He hadn't intended to be dishonest, but once trouble struck, he'd taken the low road, allowed Dr. Mann to manipulate the situation so he could save his job. Madeline understood retirement and health-benefit worries, but even if she'd had a frightened spouse and her future was on the line, she'd like to think she'd do the right thing.

The more pressing issue was what was she going to do now? She had no doubt she would get her job back... but did she want it?

Even if the job atmosphere wasn't destined to be different when she returned to work, she was different. She didn't have the same drive to do this job as she once had.

Fair or not, she couldn't have her old life back. She either had to adapt or leave. But she could also make sure Dr. Mann didn't succeed in driving her away.

After lunch at a small coffee shop that catered to students, Madeline walked to campus and into Edenton Hall, where the anthropology department was located. Dr. Vanessa Mann's secretary was still out, since it was only quarter to one, but Vanessa was in her office. Madeline walked in without knocking.

Dr. Mann glanced up from the records she was inspecting, a stunned look crossing her face when she realized who was standing on the other side of the desk.

"A word?" Madeline asked politely.

Dr. Mann nodded, glancing over Madeline's shoulder. She set the silver pen she'd been holding back in its holder and fixed her hard gaze on Madeline, who stared back impassively. The woman was going to have to do better than that, because she was dealing with someone who didn't feel she had a whole lot to lose.

"I received notice of the investigative hearing. Sixty days from now."

"Scheduling problems. It's still within the framework outlined by the university policy manual."

"I can save you a whole lot of time," Madeline said, knowing that Everett would, quite frankly, kill her if he knew what she was doing.

"How?" Dr. Mann frowned suspiciously, possibly hoping that Madeline would simply confess.

"I don't know how Dr. Jensen got the blood samples, but it wasn't from me," Madeline said, ignoring the question.

"That's for the committee to decide."

"They'll decide in my favor."

Dr. Mann allowed herself a slight smile that came off more like a sneer. "How can you be so certain?"

"Because the samples could have only been taken during that window of time when the lab was unmanned. During finals week. Your own inquiry committee agrees."

"And I suppose you have an alibi?"

"I do."

"Care to share it?" Dr. Mann said in a voice that clearly indicated she didn't think Madeline would.

"My brother died just prior to that. I spent that finals week, the one in which I was supposedly pilfering blood samples, in Maine with my grandmother, burying my brother." She cocked her head. "You need to look for another scapegoat fast, so I thought I'd give you a heads up." She smiled.

"I'm not looking for a scapegoat," Dr. Mann snapped. "I'm looking for the truth."

"Are you? Dr. Jensen brings in a lot of grant funding. I'm new to the game, so I don't. I wonder which of us is more expendable?"

"Anything else?" Dr. Mann asked coldly.

Madeline smiled without a trace of amusement. "Just one other thing."

WHEN THE PHONE RANG, Ty didn't answer. It was late. The generator was off. It went through its six rings and kicked into voice mail. Ty rolled over. The phone rang again.

Great. He got out of bed, walked unerringly down the

dark hall to the kitchen, where his cell phone glowed and vibrated on the counter.

"Hello," he practically barked into the phone.

"Ty? It's Madeline."

He knew that because his heart had hit his ribs at the sound of her voice. So much for being over her.

"I need your help."

"What kind of help?" he asked, not quite understanding why she needed his help at ten-thirty at night—one-thirty in the morning her time.

"Either a shovel or a ride. I hit the ditch halfway up the road to the ranch."

Ty stilled. "You're on the road to the ranch? Right now?"

"No. I'm off the road. In the ditch."

He closed his eyes.

"Ty, can you please come help me? You know I'll just show up if you don't come."

"Yeah, but maybe I'd have time to prepare."

"What?"

"Stay put."

She muttered, "As if I have anywhere else to go," as he put down the phone. He dressed in a hurry, since it was cold, and told Alvin to stay in the house. The stars were like diamonds in the inky sky, and the snow creaked beneath his boots. Approaching zero. Maddie had picked one hell of a night to do whatever it was she was doing.

He just hoped his heart was in one piece when she got through.

MADELINE MADE IT BACK in the rental car just as Ty's headlights appeared in the distance. She'd had to hike a good half mile down the icy road to get a cell signal, but thought she'd be back to her car well before he arrived. Apparently Ty had hurried. As soon as he stopped the truck he got out and walked over to her door before she had finished gathering her stuff together. He pulled the door open and gestured at his truck with his head, taking her suitcase from her as she went by. He didn't say a word, but when she started around the truck for the passenger side, he took her arm and helped her up through the open driver's-side door, then put the suitcase in the extended cab.

"I'm sorry," she said, once he got into the truck again. The heat blowing on her felt heavenly after the frigid walk.

"I wasn't doing anything but sleeping."

She watched his mouth tighten in profile. It stayed tight for about a mile and then he said, "What the hell are you thinking, driving alone on a road like this on a night like this?"

"I guess I was thinking I wanted to get to the ranch."

"Why?"

"Because we have matters to discuss."

"The ranch."

"That's one."

"What's the other?"

Madeline turned to stare straight ahead, sensing his quick, piercing glance, but refusing to look back. Ty had to focus on the icy, rutted road and Madeline knew he was right—what *had* she been thinking, driving on a road like this on a night like this?

Once they reached the ranch, he drove through the open gate without bothering to close it. He pulled the truck into its parking spot, yanked on the emergency brake. Even in the dim light from the dashboard, she could see his eyes were blazing.

He'd opened his mouth to speak, probably to say something that started with "What the hell," when Madeline opened her door and got out, dropping the eighteen inches to the ground.

Ty did the same, slamming his door. They marched together to his back porch, where he let her in ahead of him, sidestepping Alvin.

"I didn't mean to drive off the road," she said as she turned to face him in the dark kitchen. She could barely see him, but she was aware of everything, absolutely everything, about him. His strength, his anger.

"But you did."

"It was stupid."

"Yeah." He settled his big hands on her shoulders and Madeline felt her knees start to go a little weak. But he didn't pull her any closer.

"I actually left in time to get here just after dark. I thought I'd stay in Skip's house and then we could talk in the morning."

"What happened?" he asked, his voice coming out on a huskier note. She could feel each one of his fingers on her shoulders.

"Semi went broadside in the road. It took forever to

get the tow trucks there. They needed two." She took a half step closer to him, feeling the warmth of his hard body, feeling his tension.

Anger? Something more? "I probably shouldn't have showed up out of the blue, but...I need a place to think. To regroup. To settle stuff with myself and with you. Ty...I just had to get away."

He stilled. "What happened with the hearings?"

"I cut a deal with my department head. If she backs off, I'll keep my mouth shut about her scummy tactics to save the departmental golden goose at the expense of an innocent bystander. PR is important, you know—especially when you're looking for private funds as well as federal."

"You still have a job?"

"I have six months to decide. A sabbatical, if you will." Madeline shook her hair back. "But I know I can't work there after this. I was buying time, trying to figure out what to do without having to go through the hell of the hearings."

His hands tightened on her shoulders. "So you need a place to hide out?"

"Actually, in spite of all the stuff that went on, I feel more at peace here than I've felt anywhere else in the world."

"The ranch does that to me, too," he said softly.

"It's not the ranch, Ty. It's you."

Madeline didn't know who moved first. She thought it was Ty, but it didn't matter, because his arms were around her and her body was pressed tightly against his as his hand pushed into her hair, holding her head against his chest.

She was home.

* * * * *

COMING NEXT MONTH

Available March 8, 2011

REQUEST YOUR FREE BOOKS!

2 FREE NOVELS PLUS 2 FREE GIFTS!

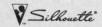

Silhouette®

ROMANTIC SUSPENSE

Sparked by Danger, Fueled by Passion.

YES! Please send me 2 FREE Silhouette® Romantic Suspense novels and my 2 FREE gifts (gifts are worth about $10). After receiving them, if I don't wish to receive any more books, I can return the shipping statement marked "cancel." If I don't cancel, I will receive 4 brand-new novels every month and be billed just $4.24 per book in the U.S. or $4.99 per book in Canada. That's a saving of at least 15% off the cover price! It's quite a bargain! Shipping and handling is just 50¢ per book in the U.S. and 75¢ per book in Canada.* I understand that accepting the 2 free books and gifts places me under no obligation to buy anything. I can always return a shipment and cancel at any time. Even if I never buy another book, the two free books and gifts are mine to keep forever.

240/340 SDN FC95

Name	(PLEASE PRINT)	
Address		Apt. #
City	State/Prov.	Zip/Postal Code

Signature (if under 18, a parent or guardian must sign)

Mail to the **Reader Service:**
IN U.S.A.: P.O. Box 1867, Buffalo, NY 14240-1867
IN CANADA: P.O. Box 609, Fort Erie, Ontario L2A 5X3

Not valid for current subscribers to Silhouette Romantic Suspense books.

Want to try two free books from another line?
Call 1-800-873-8635 or visit www.ReaderService.com.

* Terms and prices subject to change without notice. Prices do not include applicable taxes. Sales tax applicable in N.Y. Canadian residents will be charged applicable taxes. Offer not valid in Quebec. This offer is limited to one order per household. All orders subject to credit approval. Credit or debit balances in a customer's account(s) may be offset by any other outstanding balance owed by or to the customer. Please allow 4 to 6 weeks for delivery. Offer available while quantities last.

USA TODAY *bestselling author Lynne Graham*
is back with a thrilling new trilogy
SECRETLY PREGNANT, CONVENIENTLY WED

Three heroines must marry alpha males to keep
their dreams...but Alejandro, Angelo and Cesario
are not about to be tamed!

Book 1—JEMIMA'S SECRET
Available March 2011 from Harlequin Presents®.

JEMIMA yanked open a drawer in the sideboard to find Alfie's birth certificate. Her son was her husband's child. It was a question of telling the truth whether she liked it or not. She extended the certificate to Alejandro.

"This has to be nonsense," Alejandro asserted.

"Well, if you can find some other way of explaining how I managed to give birth by that date and Alfie not be yours, I'd like to hear it," Jemima challenged.

Alejandro glanced up, golden eyes bright as blades and as dangerous. "All this proves is that you must still have been pregnant when you walked out on our marriage. It does not automatically follow that the child is mine."

"'I know it doesn't suit you to hear this news now and I really didn't want to tell you. But I can't lie to you about it. Someday Alfie may want to look you up and get acquainted."

"If what you have just told me is the truth, if that little boy does prove to be mine, it was vindictive and extremely selfish of you to leave me in ignorance!"

Jemima paled. "When I left you, I had no idea that I was still pregnant."

"Two years is a long period of time, yet you made no attempt to inform me that I might be a father. I will want DNA tests to confirm your claim before I make any decision about what I want to do."

"Do as you like," she told him curtly. "*I* know who Alfie's father is and there has never been any doubt of his identity."

"I will make arrangements for the tests to be carried out and I will see you again when the result is available," Alejandro drawled with lashings of dark Spanish masculine reserve.

"I'll contact a solicitor and start the divorce," Jemima proffered in turn.

Alejandro's eyes narrowed in a piercing scrutiny that made her uncomfortable. "It would be foolish to do anything before we have that DNA result."

"I disagree," Jemima flashed back. "I should have applied for a divorce the minute I left you!"

Alejandro quirked an ebony brow. "And why didn't you?"

Jemima dealt him a fulminating glance but said nothing, merely moving past him to open her front door in a blunt invitation for him to leave.

"I'll be in touch," he delivered on the doorstep.

What is Alejandro's next move? Perhaps rekindling their marriage is the only solution! But will Jemima agree?

*Find out in Lynne Graham's
exciting new romance
JEMIMA'S SECRET*

*Available March 2011
from Harlequin Presents®.*

Start your Best Body today with these top 3 nutrition tips!

1. **SHOP THE PERIMETER OF THE GROCERY STORE:** The good stuff—fruits, veggies, lean proteins and dairy—always line the outer edges of the store. When you veer into the center aisles, you enter the temptation zone, where the unhealthy foods live.

2. **WATCH PORTION SIZES:** Most portion sizes in restaurants are nearly twice the size of a true serving and at home, it's easy to "clean your plate." Use these easy serving guidelines:
   - Protein: the palm of your hand
   - Grains or Fruit: a cup of your hand
   - Veggies: the palm of two open hands

3. **USE THE RAINBOW RULE FOR PRODUCE:** Your produce drawers should be filled with every color of fruits and vegetables. The greater the variety, the more vitamins and other nutrients you add to your diet.

Find these and many more helpful tips in

YOUR BEST BODY NOW

by

TOSCA RENO

WITH STACY BAKER

Bestselling Author of
THE EAT-CLEAN DIET®

Available wherever books are sold!

NTRSERIESFEB